ACROSS MY KNEE

A Mischief Collection of Erotica

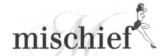

mischief

Mischief
An imprint of HarperCollins*Publishers*
77–85 Fulham Palace Road,
Hammersmith, London W6 8JB

www.mischiefbooks.com

A Paperback Original 2013

First published in Great Britain in ebook format by
HarperCollins*Publishers* 2012

A catalogue record for this book is
available from the British Library

ISBN-13: 9780007534883

Set in Sabon by FMG using Atomic ePublisher from Easypress

Find out more about HarperCollins and the environment at
www.harpercollins.co.uk/green

CONTENTS

CONTENTS

Birthday Surprise
Poppy St Vincent

'You did what?' His voice froze her with its tone.

'I just thought you'd find it ...' There did not seem to be a good end to the sentence. Marie ran a manicured hand down her new dress and thought what a terrible waste. It should have been such fun.

'She's not an "it".' He looked at his girlfriend with hard eyes, for once genuinely angry at what she had done.

She scowled. 'I never thought she was. I like her. I thought you'd like her too. I wanted you to be proud of me.'

'OK.' He sat on the sofa, leaned back and closed his eyes, then breathed in and out, just once but deeply, before he instructed her, 'Tell me what you've done.'

She sat on the floor at his feet, curled her hands around his right leg and leaned her cheek on his knee. He could not see her face as she talked but that suited her.

'It's Ali; you know Ali. You know that she's in a different department to me, accounting.' She tried to pre-empt his question. 'You know I have liked her for ages, we talked about that.' Her cheeks coloured with a blush as she remembered what she had whispered in his ear. 'Ali and I, well, we've talked before, but since my promotion things have ... developed.'

She paused and pushed her head back a little, waiting for a comforting gesture, feeling the gentle weight of his hand on her head, but none came and she continued.

'Well, you know I have to manage departments, and hers is one of them. I am her boss's boss. Her boss, Mike, is a sweet guy, and terrified of me.'

She turned and looked at him for the first time, her neat eyebrows raised in a question.

'No,' he assured her. 'I have never been scared of you. It's never going to happen. Now get on with it. We don't have a lot of time and I am going to give you a real hiding before she arrives.'

'But you can't! Not tonight! I am supposed to ... I am ...'

His eyes bore down on her. She turned away and nestled again, holding on to him tightly, continuing in a smaller and less confident voice. She knew if she argued

2

at all it would be worse for her later. Even now she could feel her façade crumbling.

* * *

It had started properly about two months before. Mike had come to see her in her new role as his boss. As he often did when he spoke to Marie, he stood slightly farther away from her desk than would be considered normal and ran a shaking hand through his short hair as he spoke.

'Do you mind if I speak to you about Ali? The thing is, she keeps coming in late, and when I speak to her about it she just laughs and says that's why I get paid more than her.'

He paused and looked wistfully at the door.

Marie tipped her head to one side, causing waves of chestnut hair to curl on one shoulder and rest on her navy suit jacket. Her brow furrowed. 'Seriously? That's what she says? And you just took that?'

'Er … yes. She thinks it's my job to cover for her. I have spoken to her, but I was wondering if you wouldn't mind, because I know you are looking over … after my department now.' Mike shifted a little on his feet. It had not occurred to either of them that he could have sat down.

Marie sighed but cut it short. 'Sure, I will sort it out.'

She looked back at her work, and refrained from saying, 'Don't let the door hit you ...' though it could not have been more obvious.

Within twenty minutes Ali was sitting across from Marie. All Marie had asked was 'How are you?' and now she was listening to a rather high-pitched account of her recent run-ins with Mike and how unfair he was. Ali had had her hair cut, a new bob, almost a pixie cut, which suited her large brown eyes and made her monologue seem almost cute to Marie, but not quite.

'We need to talk about being late,' Marie interrupted. 'About *you* being late, that is. You can't be. You also can't tell Mike that it's his job to hold the fort for you when you are. It's his job to bollock you if you're late. God knows, if you were in my department I would. And now, of course, effectively you are in my department so don't treat me as though I will let you get away with anything because I certainly won't. I would make mincemeat of you if you spoke to me like you speak to him.'

And that's when it happened. Ali opened her large brown eyes and looked up at Marie with surprise. Her olive skin took on a dusky pink hue and her lips formed a perfect round O of surprise.

Marie, who had told off plenty of adults, had never seen one react quite like this. She watched in silence as Ali transformed before her. She dipped her pretty little head as though Marie had pushed it down, her skin

4

flushed a deep pink, and her lips moved as though to form an objection that never quite appeared.

Ali's lowly posture reminded Marie of an ex-girlfriend, a very lovely girl with whom Marie had spent six months during her twenties. She remembered how she herself had responded when rebuked, the same shyness, the same almost virginal reaction. She thought also of her present lover, Ben, and how amused he would be by all this. And she saw a temptation, a possibility, and a delightful opportunity. All of these visions, ideas and possibilities came together as she watched Ali look down at her hands, which held one another on her lap.

Without missing a beat she said, 'And do you know what I would do if you were in my department? I would make it so you never even thought of being late again. My people just don't do this. You know that, don't you?'

Ali's shy smile faltered and she nodded a little, her head still dipped.

'Ali?'

The girl looked up.

'Has anyone ever told you off before? As an adult, I mean?'

Ali shook her head.

'That explains a lot. You know that I am going to be overseeing your department from now on, and if you are late again I will be the one dealing with you, so a telling off will be the least you have to worry about. I have half a mind to make you stand in the corner and think about that.'

They both laughed a quiet, insincere laugh. Ali's face was now bright pink and her eyes remained focused on the floor.

Marie dismissed her, watching the slightly awkward way Ali carried the cute dress that showed off her legs to perfection.

Marie then sat musing. She knew the look Ali had given her. She knew it because it was just the sort of look she gave Ben about twenty times a day. It was the early submission look. It was not giving in; it certainly was not the total bottom-up surrender that she always wallowed in eventually, but the surrender was there in its infancy. It was an early indicator of later success, and Ali had given it to Marie.

Later that day, she lay in bed with Ben. Her bottom was swollen and sore, and she lay carefully on her side while she pushed herself deeper into his arms.

'How come,' she asked his chest, 'at work I get to be in charge of everyone and people are nervous about me, but here I get spanked for every little thing I do wrong?'

Ben opened one lazy eye and continued drawing a circle on her shoulder. 'What exactly are you asking?'

'Why am I in charge there and not ever in charge here?'

He opened both eyes now and reached down to squeeze

her bottom. 'Do you want to be? You can't, but do you want that?'

'No.' Her voice squeaked. 'I just want to know what it's like. I just want to know how you feel sometimes. I want not always to be the one who gets spanked. I am important.' Her voice sounded thin in her own ears, and she was starting to kick a little under the covers.

Ben took her face in his hands and made her look at him. It was a forceful move and her heart thudded heavily as she met his eyes.

'Marie, you are important. And at work you can be as bossy as you like, but at home that's never going to happen. You don't even want it, do you?'

Her lips opened a little but no words were waiting there. She arched her back and tried to move her face towards his.

He looked at her for a moment more before he leaned down and kissed her. When he let her go, she pushed her whole body into his. He smiled, put her under him, and entered her with a force that made them both gasp.

At work over the next few weeks, Marie took a special interest in Ali. It made perfect sense to give her new charge a little more attention. Ali had a reputation for having a lot of promise and a terrible attitude in equal measure, and Marie compiled a list of complaints and concerns about her. Her tantrums were legendary; Mike and a few others were terrified of her outbursts, and she was known to fly off the handle at the slightest hint of an insult.

After one particularly difficult exchange that left Mike shaking in the hallway, Marie stormed into Ali's office and demanded to know what had happened, but when Ali started to explain she interrupted.

'No, Ali, just no. I asked but I am just not interested. This stops and it stops now. If we weren't at work, I'd recommend you get the spanking of your life. Your behaviour would be unacceptable in a six-year-old. Go and see Mike, and sort it out with him, because if I have to you won't like it at all.'

And she left. It was only when she reached her office that Marie realised what she had said. She started to go back and apologise but then stopped and sat at her desk instead, waiting for alarm bells to sound, for the police to run in, or whatever happens when someone says something totally unacceptable. Nothing happened. Shaking her head gently, she returned to her work.

On the other side of the building, Ali still sat where she had been when Marie burst in. Many minutes passed, and then in a tiny whisper she told the space where Marie had been, 'I wish we weren't at work.'

Time passed. Ali started to spend an inordinate amount of time wandering the corridors near Marie's office. She tried very hard to remember exactly what it was that Marie had threatened her with, wishing she could have recorded the words to replay at night when she was alone. Every memory became precious – the furious way Marie had opened her door, the way Marie's eyes had honed in on her, the words she used, but mostly the terrifying, hope-giving threat. She oscillated between being the perfect minion and the most awful harridan because she wanted Marie to be proud of her and furious with her in turn.

Eventually, she persuaded herself that it was all a myth, that Marie had said nothing of the kind to her, because no one had ever spoken to her like that. No one ever would, no one would ever dare. The thought made her furious, and that was how it happened.

A short while after this horrible realisation, Ali burst into Marie's office with neither warning nor a knock, and plopped down in the chair facing Marie's desk.

'I have to talk to you,' she said.

'Evidently so.' Marie responded, then took a moment to survey Ali. Her hair was messy, as if she had run her hands through it. Her shoulders were up, and her large eyes were filled with unshed tears.

'Mike is a prick. Do you know what he did? The bloody idiot –'

Marie raised a hand. 'Stop talking.' She spoke as if Ali were a young child, her voice heavy and even. 'I want you to think through what you want to say to me before you say another word. I am not going to sit here and listen to a tantrum. If you really want to risk it, then go ahead, but you won't like the consequences.'

Ali glared, to no effect since Marie had already turned away to continue her work. So she kicked the floor a couple of times, the edge of her shoe catching on the chair leg. She looked at the door, opened her mouth three times, then sat on her hands. Her breathing steadied.

Minutes passed.

'Yesterday,' she started, and Marie turned and to look, 'Mike came to see me and told me that he had given the Stirwick report to Charles. I really wanted that project and I've been here for ages more than Charles. I have more experience than him, and I am better at my job than him. It's just jobs for the bloody boys, isn't it?'

'Did you do anything about this feeling you have?' Marie asked quietly.

'Yes, I bloody well did. I went to Mike, and Charles was there of course, because they are bosom buddies now, and told him what a jerk he was, Mike that is. And I told Charles that he can sod off too.'

Marie put her head on one side as Ali spoke. She took in every word of Ali's tirade, and for the first time in her six years of knowing him, she pitied Mike.

'Ali, you need to stop talking now. Mike asked me about the Stirwick project and I suggested Charles should do it. I could explain the reasoning to you, but, quite frankly, I don't want to. Your behaviour today has been unprofessional and histrionic. Leave my office now, and we will talk about this when I have had a chance to think about how best to deal with it. But I think we both know what you deserve, don't we?'

She turned away from Ali in cold dismissal.

After thirty long seconds, Ali left. She walked to the loo, locked herself in a cubicle and cried. 'Stupid, stupid cow,' she hissed, and tried with all her self-deception skills to pretend she was talking about Marie.

* * *

That night was the monthly session where the girls from several departments would meet and have a few drinks. It often ended up being quite a raucous affair for those girls that wanted it to be.

Ali was there and on fine form. She cracked jokes, and responded with shrieks of delight when Marie joined the party, which Marie did her best to ignore. Wine flowed, a couple of cocktails were quaffed, the conversation got louder, and everyone forgot about work. It may have been the drink, or the atmosphere, or even a desire to push Marie's buttons, but a couple of times when Ali sat down she shoved the table and almost sent glasses and bottles flying.

Each time she did it, the girls all flew to save their drinks and their outfits, and annoyance with her grew rapidly.

'Oh, for God's sake,' Mel snapped, 'just watch what you're doing.'

'I can't, I have a table leg, look!' Ali pointed and gently rattled the table. 'You can't do anything else with a little skirt and a table leg. You can all bugger off.' She laughed and toasted them by draining half a glass of red wine.

Marie waited until the next violent shake, and said in as stern a voice as she could manage, 'Ali, I swear if you do that again I shall spank you.'

The whole table broke up into giggles, except for Ali. She blushed furiously but her half-laugh provided enough cover for the group not to notice. Marie, thrilled by the effect her words had had and keen to take further ground, desperately tried to decide what Ben would say next.

She followed her remark with what she hoped was a meaningful glance and a single, bright-red nail pointed at Ali's nose. 'Next time. I mean it.' With a smile that could have meant anything, she then turned from Ali and asked the girl to her left just what it is about Radley bags that make them so addictive.

'Why on earth did I need to think of Ben?' Marie inwardly grumbled. 'I can do this myself. If I were at work, I would not even think of asking him anything. I have to get a grip. I need my desk and my work head.'

Neither girl dared look at the other for several minutes. Marie felt uncertain that she could carry off her new game, and did not dare to check her progress. Ali was blushing, trying not to knock the table, and fighting such conflicted feelings that she felt on the edge of panic, which she covered with a smile so wide she thought her face would crack.

Marie was somewhat surprised when Ali accepted her offer of a lift home, but it gave Marie a clear indication that she could carry on with her plan. While driving, Marie swore quietly to herself and wished she could ring Ben to find out what to do.

It is all very well knowing what the man should do to make you feel terribly submissive, she thought, but how scary it is to do it. What if she just tells me to go away?

When she was at work, it was so easy to be in charge. She knew how to reduce anyone to a little piece of himself, and then build him back up to be confident and capable. But once in a home environment, she felt like a little girl playing with toys.

She listened to Ali's pitter pat of chatter as they wove down dark lanes, and knew that Ali was feeling the quirk of submission. Marie recognised the signs of a girl who did not dare let there be silence for fear what might happen in it. It was just how she was with Ben in their early months together. Orange light rose and fell on Ali's face as they drove out of town, and Marie enjoyed the way Ali's lipstick looked almost black in the light.

She knew the way and drove the tiny one-track lane

to Ali's house without instructions. Marie parked and waited only a momentted.

Marie smiled, and hoped her heart did not sound as loud to Ali as it did to her. 'Well, I shall then,' she said, feeling, for reasons she did not quite understand, like the fox in a fairy story.

* * *

Marie leaned back on the sofa and crossed her legs, and was glad she had worn stockings. Ben preferred them, of course, but since she was on her own she had considered not bothering. Ali sat by her feet and had gathered up the courage to gently stroke her ankle, fingertips rolling up and down her ankle, a timid touch, a preamble.

'I'm sorry about today.'

Marie shifted a little in her seat. 'Ali, I like you so much, but you were awful. You really were. I don't understand why you lose control like that. It's as if you have everything going for you, but you just decide to throw it away.'

Ali sat still, her finger resting on the buckle of Marie's high-heeled shoe.

'All I wanted to do today was spank you, Ali, and that's why I sent you away. I wanted to spank you and then I wanted to kiss you, both of which are not really things I should do at work.' She smiled weakly, her heart pounding.

'I wish you would.'

She swallowed dryness and surged on. 'The thing is, I am in love, and you know Ben. He is quite –' her eyes searched the ceiling for a word '– assertive, and there is nothing I don't share with him, nothing at all.' She let the moment rest. Somewhere the house creaked, as though approving her confession.

Ali nodded slowly, looking only at the shoe before her. 'I like Ben. I like him a lot. He spoke to me at the Christmas party, and lots of us have crushes on him. I do, I guess. He's a bit scary though. Except I think I like that.' The final part was a whisper too quiet to be heard unless by ears that wished to hear it. 'But you,' she continued, 'you can be scary too. When you are like you are at work, I feel better about myself. I feel safe. Well, not today. I felt crappy about today, and I still do.'

She looked up at Marie.

Marie leaned down and they kissed. Her lips are so soft, Marie thought, her whole self is open to me, and she is waiting for me to act. I want to be the girl who acts. I can be that girl with her.

Ali wore a softer expression now than Marie was used to seeing. She looked expectant, hopeful, shy. She looked, Marie realised, like a girl who hoped to be taken somewhere and did not quite know where.

Everything was as new for Marie as it was for Ali. She was so used to Ben's hard body, the trim, businesslike shape of a male, his hands that held her, and his lips that were unrelenting and demanding. But Ali's lips parted and welcomed her while they kissed. They responded to her desire, trembled and followed Marie's every lead. The girls stood, and Marie felt Ali yield, felt the way Ali waited for her, arms hanging at her sides. Marie reached up and tilted Ali's head, surprised and empowered by her ability to manoeuvre another human being. She stepped forward and pushed Ali back against the wall, her kisses becoming more urgent and demanding.

Ali made a little noise almost of distress, but Marie knew it was not. It was the sound of wanting that is not quite ready, the sound of desire that wants to be forced to wait, to hold on to itself. Marie had made that sound a thousand times, and she knew this was the time to explore where she could take this pretty, hopeful girl and her desire that was not yet desire.

It was intoxicating. Marie had been given the keys to the castle while the lord was away. For once, it was all about what she wanted, and what she decided. Ali's breasts rose and fell sharply, and Marie knew how strong her need had grown. She slipped a hand into Ali's dress and reached for a hard nipple, and with one thumb she encircled the tip, kissing Ali gently until she could feel Ali almost break with wanting.

But still Ali needed to feel the desire more than the release.

Marie knew what she herself wanted, and she knew she could have it. For once, everything would be just as she determined. She did not have to guess or hope; she could instruct and create. She looked into Ali's expectant eyes, and saw them sadden as she pulled away.

Marie walked to the centre of the room, her heels announcing themselves on the wooden floor.

'Come here,' she commanded.

To her amazement, Ali did. She walked carefully, taking each step as if a thousand men looked on. But it was only Marie in front of the girl, waiting in barely hidden amazement to receive her.

Ali stood just where Marie had chosen. Her shoulders were square but her eyes were down, and a gentle blush spread across her cheeks, like a doll, or a design in a computer model. Marie knew what she wanted.

'Turn around.' Marie watched the confusion in Ali's eyes as she obeyed. Her feet shuffled as she turned; she was clearly unsure and so wanted to show unwillingness, and both girls were taken aback by her compliance.

Marie smiled at the girl's back, and reached up and unzipped Ali's dress. Goose bumps formed on Ali's shoulders. She was glorious in black satin and stockings, and Marie stared, ran her fingers down Ali's back, watching carefully as Ali shivered at her touch. The sight of the girl's underwear brought a powerful throbbing of desire through Marie. Ali had wanted this all along. She dressed for the evening with the desire to be unwrapped.

I can do anything, Marie thought, and this is how it feels. She almost laughed with delight.

'I want you to learn to do as I say,' she whispered, her red lips almost touching Ali's tiny ear. 'I want you to learn how to mind me, before we move on to other things. I think you would love to spend time with Ben, wouldn't you? Aren't you curious about what it's like with him? About how it feels with him?'

Ali used every ounce of her concentration to keep herself upright, to maintain an illusion of control.

Without saying a word, Marie abandoned Ali, sat on the sofa and watched the young woman. Could it be that Ali would stay there until she told her to move? Was that possible? What would she do if Ali moved? She suddenly wished Ben were there, just for a moment, until she saw Ali's hand reach around to cover her bottom. She felt self-conscious, and Marie knew the feeling well. She also knew what Ben would say.

'Stay still.' Her voice sounded authoritative to both of them.

Ali stopped. Marie could have clapped but knew that would spoil the picture.

Marie's heart beat so hard that she could see her dress bounce against her chest. Could she do this? Did she have the nerve? She wanted to. She wanted to know how it felt.

18

'Ali, come and stand by me. Just here, to my right.'
She pointed.

Ali's face was the image of regret and anticipation,
presented to Marie as Ali fought to obey. With tiny geisha
steps Ali crossed the room. It was only a short distance,
but submission always feels farther than it is.

'Over my lap please.' Oh bugger. Should she have said
'please'? She tried to remember if Ben ever said please.
She pondered this as Ali slowly leaned forward over her
lap. Willing her hands to stop shaking, Marie stroked
Ali's knickers as they spread over round curves. The dark,
smooth material stretched under her hand as she moved
it down the centre of Ali's bum. It was a subtle move
but Marie knew just what Ali felt. She knew how much
Ali wanted her to act; she was walking the bridge between
fear and anticipation. They both were. Very slowly, with
care not to let Ali feel her shake, Marie lowered Ali's
knickers. Her bum was beautiful. Marie cupped her hand
over it. It was round, pert and perfect. It was so pale
that all Marie wanted in the world was to bring colour
to it.

'I know how you feel about today, and this is for that
feeling, for both of us, because we both know you earned
it.'

She raised her hand and brought it down sharply. Ali
made a little cry, but it was only surprise, and Marie
wanted to hear more than that. Cupping her hand she

set to work, and for several minutes she peppered Ali's little bum with spanks. It turned light pink, and Ali moved a little, a tiny squirm, but it was not enough. Marie knew what she felt. It was embarrassment, but more than that it was impatience. Marie tried harder and used more force; she spanked as hard as she could, up and over the waiting globes. She wanted more. She wanted to do more. She wanted to hear a peal of distress. She listened. She heard a little sound but she recognised it as encouragement. She did not want encouragement, she wanted Ali to wonder why she had asked for such a thing, she wanted Ali to mind her, to feel an edge of regret for what she had got into.

Marie stopped and thought. What would hurt? What would make her put her hands back and try to make me stop?

She reached down into her bag and found a small paddle hairbrush. She knew this hurt, because she had felt its impact countless times.

Ali called out at the first slap, but Marie ignored her and went for all she was worth. From the top of Ali's thighs she worked up and down the bottom. The colours that blossomed fascinated her as, over and over, she covered the bottom in quick, hard pops. She felt the most powerful thrill, and it was all her choice. She did not ever want to stop, but did all that she wanted to; she remembered the sit spot; she remembered how much it hurt when the same spot was focused on; she remembered how it felt not to be able to predict pace or position. Everything she had learned on the receiving end, she used in that spanking.

And then she heard it. She heard Ali struggling, really struggling to accept what was being done to her. Marie did not stop. She wanted more, and she took everything she wanted. I am not the girl I normally am, she thought. I am the girl in charge now. I can do anything.

At last, exhausted, she quit. Her breath came quick, and she felt invigorated. She looked at the bottom before her, a little horrified at its condition.

But then she remembered. She was in charge now. She could do what she liked. There was no need to be horrified; it was not her bottom.

'Stand in the corner. No rubbing.'

And she watched, enthralled, as Ali stiffly and slowly stood, and hobbled to the corner by the window.

Marie shook her head in disbelief, then sat for half an hour and watched and wondered at what she had done.

Then she stood and walked over to the girl in the corner, the girl who was not her, and whispered into her ear. 'In one week's time you will come to our house. It is my Ben's birthday. You will come dressed as you were tonight, and you will do what you are told when you arrive. Do you understand?'

21

Her voice was gentle, like honey in warm summer woods.

Ali nodded.

'Good girl.'

Marie kissed her shoulder gently, took her bag and left.

When she had gone, Ali walked stiffly to her room. She stood for several minutes staring in the mirror at her bruised and swollen bottom. She stroked it with her head to one side, a gentle hand where before there had been only pain.

Is this how it is? she wondered. Is this how it is to be punished? She sighed. 'I thought there would be more.' But more of what, she could not, or would not, think.

* * *

Marie finished telling her side of the story to Ben, not once daring to turn around and look at him, like a successful Orpheus.

'I am beginning to understand now,' said Ben, bringing Marie back to the present. 'It would have been a good idea to talk to me about this in advance, don't you think?'

'I know,' she said to the rug, 'that this is a bit unusual, but you've been in charge of me for years, and I have been spanked so often and in so many ways that I wanted to know how it felt. I wanted to show you. I wanted –'

she struggled with the final bit of truth '– I wanted to kiss her, like you kiss me. I wanted to share that with you.'

She paused, and the silence rang in her ears.

'Did I screw up?' she asked at last.

The room was heavy with waiting. All the power she had felt while she recounted the story dissipated and flew like a butterfly to Ben's finger while she waited for his verdict.

'I can't believe that you did all of this without asking me, and, more importantly, without really thinking through the effect it would have on Ali.'

His displeasure made her sit up and search for a way to make it better.

'But I did, we talked about it, I just didn't tell you everything because I didn't want you to know about the surprise. It's supposed to be a happy thing. Ali has always liked you, ever since she met you at the Christmas party three years ago. She thinks you're gorgeous, and she told me. I do too. Two women who think you're gorgeous, what's not to love about that?'

Marie finished with a smile, and Ben tapped the edge of the chair with his fingers.

'OK,' he said.

'OK? Really? So it's all good?'

'Oh.' He looked down at the brown-haired girl, still under his hand. 'No, not yet. I wasn't really talking to you. Get your hairbrush and come back here.'

23

She started to speak.

'Now.'

Flustered at his curt interruption, she dashed off to do as instructed. Her skirt flew up as she ran, and he smiled a little at the flash of stockings and black silk knickers.

Marie returned with hairbrush and excuses in hand. 'Ben, I spent ages getting ready. I tried really hard to do whatever I ... oh.'

He sat just pointing at his lap. They watched each other for a moment and Marie lost. She folded herself over his thighs without a word, and lifted up her bum so he could pull her knickers down.

'Jesus!' she called out as he unleashed the hairbrush with force over her pale cheeks. 'Ben!' She tried desperately to get away but his arm clamped her tightly. 'You haven't warmed me up and it really hurts!'

He responded with a totally unfazed and unaltered assault on her bum. She tried to crawl away using the edge of the sofa for purchase but he held her still with his non-spanking arm and went to work with tenacity over all her bottom and thighs.

She heard it stop before she felt it. Her bottom burned and Marie groaned with relief, then realised Ben was speaking to her and resolved to listen to him dutifully.

'Right, listen very carefully to this, Marie. You don't know what you are doing, do you? I know you. You feel all of this, you don't think it. You have taken this girl somewhere. Why? What did you want? What did you think about her and how she felt? And did you think about who is in charge of all this? Did you?' He punctuated each syllable of the last two questions with a hard swat of the brush that made her cry out each time.

The doorbell rang. He paused, the brush in mid-air, and she waited, eyes squeezed tight shut for a number of reasons, none of them that she dared consider.

'Get up.'

She scrambled to readjust her clothes, trying to look dignified and normal for their guest.

He looked at her with stern bemusement. 'What are you doing?' He did not wait for an answer. 'Get into the corner, knickers down, skirt up, and don't even think about moving before I tell you to.'

The confidence the man had in his authority was such that he did not wait to see her carry out his orders, but went straight to the front door and then ushered Ali to the kitchen.

After only a few minutes, Marie started to feel a little less fear, and leaned backwards to try to hear what was being said. It was unkind and inconsiderate of him to put her into the corner when Ali arrived. He showed no respect at all for her position.

She could hear only muffled voices from the kitchen, and felt ignored and bypassed. Why couldn't they discuss it with her? Why didn't her feelings count? She was the one who had orchestrated this, after all.

It will be so confusing and bewildering for Ali, Marie thought, and it would be fairer for everyone if I put myself to rights and joined them, like a normal person.

Then she heard footsteps approaching and recognised Ben's steady tread, and almost slammed her nose into the wall in her haste to get back into position.

Ben stood right behind her, his fingers carelessly stroking her exposed and still sore bum as he spoke. His voice sounded deep and certain in her ear, and in another situation it would have turned her on, listening to him speak so deeply and so close to her, but right then she was too frantic about Ali being there for that to happen.

'I have had a conversation with Ali. She and I have spoken about how she feels and what she wants. I also know what I want. Pull your knickers up and come out of the corner. Sit on this.' He plonked a chair in the middle of the floor. 'Right. Spank her. Let's see how you do.'

Marie had pulled her knickers up before he finished that fragment of his sentence but she stood still, looking from the chair to him and then to Ali. Her stomach fell and she did not know why. This is what she wanted all along, but in front of him it felt stupid all of a sudden, as if she were a child playing at a silly game.

'If you need me to show you how it's done, I can

spank you before you spank her,' he offered, noting the forlorn and hopeless look on her face.

Something in Marie snapped to attention and she turned to face a rather less compliant Ali than she had seen the other night. She searched for her work voice and hoped she had located it as she declared to Ali, 'Right then, young lady, let's finish what we started last week.'

Ali stood and stared, her chin jutted out in a way that Marie had not seen before, and her stance somewhat relaxed, but also somewhat 'come and get me if you think you are hard enough'. Marie paused for just a second, ignoring Ben as best she could, then took Ali's wrist and sat on the chair as she yanked the girl over her lap. It was an undignified landing and Ali grunted softly as her stomach hit Marie's thighs, but in a moment they were sorted out, Ali's skirt was up and her knickers at half-mast.

Marie felt more confidence then, which was impressive considering the pain in her bum and how having a woman, even a petite one, over her lap made that swollen bum feel even less comfortable. She tried to think of something Toppy to say, but Ben would know she was nicking all his lines so she resorted to action.

Slapping sounds soon filled the room, but that was all. Marie did her best to light a fire in Ali's bottom, and she knew she was getting some good ones in but it simply was not having an impact. Ali glared at the floor and, although Marie could not see her eyes, she knew how little effect she was having. She redoubled her efforts and tried with all she was worth to draw even a small squeal from Ali, but there was nothing. A sinking feeling grew in her stomach until suddenly she was reminded why Ali had been in trouble at work in the first place.

'Oh, for God's sake,' the girl declared, 'my grandmother can spank harder than that and she's been dead five years.'

Marie heard Ben's snort, which was rich considering that, if she had said that over his lap, she would have to write a letter of condolence to her own bottom. She looked down at the light pink globes and realised she was sunk. She did not have anywhere to take it.

'God,' she moaned, 'you can be such a little bitch at times.'

She spanked harder as she lost her temper. She had tried so hard, planned so well, and it had felt so good the other night, that it was beyond thoughtless of the other two not to help her. The frustration and confusion she felt poured out of her hands and on to Ali's darkening bottom.

Ali felt the loss of control, felt the change of tempo and dynamic, and twisted herself off Marie's lap, landing in a heap on the floor.

'A bitch? Seriously? Me? Have you even considered

what you're like?' She stood and glared, and Marie stood to meet her eye to eye.

Neither had seen the other like this. Marie's poise and confidence from work had flown from her, and Ali's compliance and eagerness to please had gone the same way. With their roles gone, it felt less like a journey into submission and more like a battle of wills.

Ben recognised the signs in Marie that he knew preceded a vitriolic blow-up, and decided enough was enough.

'My turn, I think.' His deep, calm voice made both women turn, and he took Ali's hand and pulled her firmly down over his knee as he sat in the chair Marie had vacated. 'You.' He barely glanced at Marie. 'Corner.'

Marie, so fired up she could barely speak, uttered an indiscriminate sound of anger and searched for words to refuse him, but then she saw for the first time how Ben looked when he spanked a girl. She watched his strong forearm pump up and down in a measured and methodical manner. She watched the way his head bent over his task, and how futile and tiny Ali's protests sounded.

She stripped down her knickers and put her nose to the corner and wondered, 'Why couldn't I get her to make a noise like that?'

But inside she knew the answer, she knew it as surely as she knew what she was, with her nose poking into the familiar corner of the room and her bottom still sore behind her.

She listened as the sounds from Ali grew urgent and distressed, almost angry, and how they journeyed to fearful, to weepy, and then to just little noises of pain.

She had not realised how vocal it was, how much a girl gives away when she is spanked.

It was a novel all of its own, she thought. This is the sound of submission. She knew she was not destined to create that sound in another.

It was as though Ben had heard her because at that moment he took the totally pliant and repentant Ali to the dining table and bent her gently over it. She started to panic and he put a warm hand on the small of her back while he instructed Marie to come and put herself next to Ali.

She obeyed, bending over the table one space to Ali's right.

Ben left the room and the girls did not look at each other, but Marie whispered, 'Are you OK?' to Ali, who replied very softly, 'Yes.'

Neither girl dared look back when Ben returned but when they heard the swishing sound they knew what he brought with him.

'Ali.' She jumped when he said her name and clenched her bum. 'I think it only fair that Marie get the first set of these, don't you agree?'

He did not wait for a response and Marie made a

little 'o' of horror with her mouth before the first burning stripe bit. She did her best to be brave and not show Ali how much it hurt, but by number four she was begging him to stop. At six he did.

'Your turn, Ali,' he declared.

Ali had no idea what to expect, but Marie's sobs told her that she should be afraid. He gave her three. At each stripe Ali shrieked and pushed her neat, tanned frame harder into the table, as if to slide through the wood and escape.

Ben went on, six more for Marie and three more for Ali, while the girls marked under his tutelage, while they altered. They pushed together on the table, holding hands, hot twisting fingers intertwined for support, and Ben knew he had done his job.

'What is it you really wanted, girls? What is it you wanted to know? To explore?' He knew the answer, of course. He knew Marie better than anyone, and Ali had told him all he needed in the kitchen.

The women struggled with themselves, then they looked into the other's tear-muddled eyes and, still bent over the table, their red, marked bottoms facing him, they kissed.

'I want to take you to bed,' Marie whispered. It was a question, a plea, a hope, to Ali, to Ben, and to herself. 'I want you to come too.'

Ben waited and looked at Ali, who held Marie's hand

and nodded, not quite looking up at him, but he could see the smile on her lips.

* * *

Ben lay on his side and watched at first.

The girls covered each other, their hands flew across the other's skin like birds in mid-flight, tracing the currents and following a pattern of longing that only the other could know. They barely stopped kissing for breath, hands finding every tiny part, all questions answered. They knew how it felt to be touched. They knew where to travel so lightly that it was hardly a whisper, and where to insist deeper and more.

Marie's head lowered, kissing Ali's breasts and stomach and farther, seeking the place that would make her gasp and forget herself. She gave Ben a knowing look as she took Ali over the brink, and Ben held Ali safe as she bucked and came; a moment then of still, of calm and quiet, Ali still breathing hard, and Marie still eager and insistent.

That was when the movement changed; stroking, pushing hair away from eyes, fingertips tracing lips, and seeking the third. His hard body came between the two, his penis stiff and welcome.

Inquisitive lips and nuzzling mouths journeyed over one another and over him, wrapped their tongues around him, girls finding each other and him, in turn, and all at once.

Ben placed Marie above Ali, on her knees, a familiar posture. He entered her from behind, watching the cane marks on her bum as he held it, putting himself gently in and up to the hilt, pulling her to him in a gentle rhythm. Ali lay underneath, watching in awe.

She touched Marie persistently, delicately. Her light fingers fluttered in Marie's folds as she leaned up to take one nipple in her mouth and then the other. Ben was above them both, slow and steady, building the pace until Marie started to break.

She cried out as she came and it was too much; she could not cope with the intensity, but Ben held tightly to her hips and completed into her.

Afterwards, lying down, a pile of warm, languid lovers, two of them said, 'Happy birthday, Ben.'

'Well, yes, it really is. And you,' he said, and kissed Marie lightly on the nose, 'are a rubbish Top. I think Ali needs someone a bit more forceful.'

He smiled as he fell asleep surrounded by lovers.

An Occasion
Sommer Marsden

'I was looking for you!' I said.

My husband Chuck cocked an eyebrow at me and smiled. 'Figured I'd headed for the hills, Alice? Run off into the wild blue yonder?'

'The mall is not that bad,' I said, dropping to a stone bench by the fountain. Or, as Chuck called it, the give-us-free-money water exhibit. The bottom was studded with silver and copper. I watched a row of toddlers guided by their harried mother walk along the edges to spy the coins.

'The mall is the ninth circle of hell,' he said, dropping down next to me. 'But we might as well do a check to make sure we got everything on the list so we don't have to come back. *Ever.*'

I snorted, rolling my eyes. 'You first.'

Chuck rifled in the bag and then pulled it wide. 'Three pairs of dress socks, a package of running socks, new stone-coloured chinos, a button-down blue shirt to replace the one you stole from me.'

'Borrowed,' I interjected.

'Stole. Oh, and a new shaving kit for that trip in January.'

'Good job!' I said it in my best kindergarten-teacher voice and he nudged me with his leg. 'My turn.'

Various bags sat stacked around my feet. 'New pyjamas for the pair you shrank.'

'Machine malfunction.'

'You shrank them.'

Chuck shook his head and peered into my next bag. 'New panties, new hose, a black sweater for next week when the board of education does its tour.'

'Are you in mourning?'

'No, I feel stronger in black,' I said.

'Makes sense. And ...'

'And what?'

'And you bought something you weren't supposed to. I can see it on your face,' he said.

I fingered the small sterling silver lightning bolt at my throat. 'It was on my birthday list. But I couldn't wait,' I said and showed him.

Chuck's nice kissable mouth narrowed down to a harsh line and he said, 'I guess I can call and tell them to put the one they're holding for me back on the shelf.'

Damn.

* * *

'I'm sorry. I'm sorry, I didn't know.' I had to run to keep up with him, almost.

Chuck walked at his normal fast clip but with a bit of anger behind it, and it was damn near impossible to keep up with him.

'You wrote it on your list, Alice. I've asked you so many times to not –'

'I know! To not buy something I've put on my list and you're right and I'm sorry but I was in the store and it was there and I'm about to turn forty and I thought I'd treat myself and ... I just ... forgot.'

Chuck turned to me, our bags rustling together as we stood almost eye to eye thanks to my three-inch boot heels. November wind whipped a piece of my hair around his face as if I were stroking him.

'You forgot?' he said, his voice so low it was snatched away by another gust.

My stomach twisted with nerves and I shifted my body from a surge of guilt. 'Yes,' I whispered.

'Really?'

I eyed the toes of my black suede boots and clenched my fists against that free-fall feeling in my gut. 'No. I knew it was on the list and I bought it because I have no patience.'

'Thank you,' he said, walking again. We were almost at the car and I felt terrible – therefore I scampered to keep up with him, though that wasn't usually my nature.

'For what?' I asked, exasperated.

'For at least being honest.'

He popped our trunk and dropped his bags inside. Then, ever the gentleman, he took my bags one by one and tucked them in the dark depths.

'We met during a lightning storm. And it's one of my fondest memories,' I babbled, trying to make amends.

What an idiot I was. Of course one of the things he'd be sure to get me was the lightning bolt. For the very same reasons I'd been impatient.

'Which is why I wanted to get it for you.'

'I'm sorry,' I said finally.

'Get in the car.' He walked me around and opened the door.

The wind scattered and tossed my hair again and as I moved past him I kissed him gently, mumbling against his firm mouth, 'I'm sorry.'

'I know you are, babe. But you still have to pay.'

* * *

All the way home I shifted. I smoothed my skirt, crossed my legs and tightened the belt of my big warm coat. I twirled my hair and watched Chuck out of my peripheral vision, but I could *not* bring myself to ask him what he meant.

I thought I knew. And I was both horrified and excited. Once upon a time after a party, I'd spilled a whole bottle of good wine. One thing had led to another and there had been a spanking. For me. Followed quickly by a fuck like no other we'd ever had.

We hadn't done it again. I don't know why. But now it hung in the air like a heavy scent.

That's where this was going.

Another small rush of fluid escaped my cunt, making my panties wet. It was pretty clear how my body felt about it. I just wasn't sure of my mind.

'It looks nice by the way,' he said when we got closer to home.

'What does?' My mind had been going a mile a minute. I was lost in a fog of my own thought.

At the red light he turned a little and pressed his fingertip over the small lightning bolt, pressing it against and slightly into my skin. 'This. It's going to look even better when it's the only thing you're wearing. That and a whole lot of red skin.'

Judging by the sound that slipped out of me at that moment, my mind was as on board with his plan as my body.

The rest of the car ride home was impossibly long. A

molasses drip of time that made me clench my finger with anticipation.

Chuck unloaded – gallant as ever – while I tried to unlock the door with trembling fingers. Inside, our bags hit the hardwood floor with a rustling protest and he turned to me, pressing in close, and said, 'Take everything off but the necklace.'

My mouth popped open – I assumed I had something to say – and yet I said nothing. My hands warred restlessly with one another in front of me.

Chuck locked the door and, when he found me standing perfectly still, he put his big hands – familiar and loved and, yes, about to spank me, I assumed – on my shoulders and physically turned me. 'Go,' he said, patting my ass and prompting me on.

I shuffled forward, my boots feeling more like concrete blocks strapped to my feet than fashionable footwear. Trudging up the stairs, I came up with a thousand and one arguments against what was about to happen. And yet, when I stripped my silk panties free of my body, they were not damp. They were soaked.

My pussy clenched and unclenched as if on the verge of orgasm as I waited. Tom Petty was right, the waiting is the hardest part. So I counted the tiles that ran along the top of our bedroom wall. Imported Italian tiles that had a design in the perfect shade of cobalt blue. We'd found them when –

'Ready, Alice?'

I hadn't heard him coming and I jumped, clutching at my throat, at the contraband small silver charm that had started this all. But I felt a throbbing pulse in my neck, my ears, my cunt.

'I ... can't we ... I could return it!' I blurted.

He chuckled, undoing his sensible maroon tie and kicking off his expensive leather loafers. 'No, we can't. I don't do make-believe and I won't pretend you didn't do it. I mean, how many honest-to-goodness requests do I make of you?'

'Not many.'

'And hasn't that always been ... what shall we call it?' He put his tie on the tie rack in his closet, his shoes neatly in line with the others. He shucked his button-down and his slacks.

'Pet peeve?' I sighed.

Chuck nodded. 'Good choice. Hasn't the birthday/ Christmas list thing always been a pet peeve of mine? If you put it on the list you don't –'

'– buy it,' I finished softly.

He walked to me with slow measured steps. Silent like a fucking ninja is my husband. He kneed my legs apart and clinically reached between my trembling legs and pushed a single finger into me. 'You are extremely wet, Alice.'

I nodded, blushing.

'But you're still trying to get out of it.'

Another shrug and I stared at my bare toes on the coffee-coloured rug. Our room was chilly and my nipples spiked with the chill. Chuck stripped off his underwear.

'Kneel,' he said.

Cock in hand, he touched the tip of himself to one nipple and then the other.

I waited, I watched, his extremely warm smooth skin brushing my chilly flesh. He stood straighter, moved closer, rubbed himself on my bottom lip and said, 'Open.'

I opened my mouth, sighing as I did it, and let him slide his erection past my lips and over my tongue. He held my head in his hands, thrusting slowly, fucking my mouth as a flurry of butterflies filled my belly and more moisture slipped from my body.

He only did it for a second and when he pulled free of my mouth I had to force myself not to chase after him with my lips.

'I think, if you tell the truth, you want it.' Chuck stared me down, pressed his finger to my lightning bolt.

A shiver coursed through me and goosebumps rose on my thighs and breasts.

'I want it but I'm desperately anxious.' It was hard to admit but I made myself.

We were close and honest and I loved him more than anything. I told him the truth even when it made me uncomfortable.

He nodded, brushed my hair back and said, 'So we'll get on with the spanking.'

'But it's my birthday soon!' I blurted, fear lancing through my belly. As if that were the most logical argument.

'What better reason then? It's an occasion.' He smiled and pointed to our bed. 'On your knees. Forty is a big milestone. I think we need to do it up right. Ten hard, ten soft, ten hard, ten soft.'

I gaped at him. 'Forty blows?'

'You're right,' he said, taking my hand and helping me stand. 'I forgot the one for luck.'

Chuck turned me and nudged the back of my legs with his knee. I buckled to the bed and put my ass in the air. Visions of our first and only spanking ricocheted through my mind. The sound of it, the feel of his hand striking my flesh, the sparkling pain bleeding into the dull throbbing pleasure. And the fucking after … oh, God.

His fingers slipped back inside me while another one touched my clit. 'Your mouth says no, Alice. But your pussy says yes.'

When he said *pussy*, when he talked bluntly to me, it did something to me. My cunt gripped up around his fingers and my eyes shut tight. I wanted to come so bad but knew I had miles to go before that happened.

'We'll start with hard.'

I braced myself but what came was a big maddening yawn of time. Nothing.

Chuck touched my ass with a soft caress from the base of my spine to the bottom of my cheek and back up again. A smoothing lulling stroke that had my muscles turning to butter.

Until the gentle touch vanished, and his hand came down.

The crack split my hearing before I actually felt it and then fire nestled in my skin. Tiny tentacles of pain spread out to my lower back, my flanks, the backs of my thighs. I had no time to catch my breath before the next blow landed. It streaked pain across the other side and now both halves of me ached. A balanced blaze of pain that stole my breath.

Blows three and four landed and my cunt seized up around nothing even as the flaring pain made my knees shake. I reminded myself these were the hard blows and soft would come next. I held on to that, clutching the sheets in my fingers as the next two were laid across my fiery skin.

'Here we go, seven and eight,' Chuck said, but, instead of landing them, he trailed a fingertip down my ass crack; finding the unyielding ring of my anus, he pressed enough to send another flare of anxiety through me.

I tensed and relaxed when he withdrew. When I relaxed, he dropped the final four spanks in quick succession, muttering to himself as he did.

Then there was silence. A great vacuum where nothing

43

existed but the rush of blood in my ears. The torturous pain bled into dully throbbing pleasure, my pussy picking up the tempo of my heart. I moaned, hair hanging in my face. I felt him sit, the bed dipping just a bit with his weight.

'Stand up, Alice.'

I stood on legs so weak they felt made of water and air.

He smiled. 'Come on. Come to me.' He sat at the foot of our bed – sitting up straight and proper, knees together, feet on the floor. He was big and handsome and muscular. A sweep of sandy hair over his forehead and impossibly dark-brown eyes. He watched me and I felt ridiculously naked. Whatever lay beyond naked, that was how I felt.

When I finally stood before him, he said, 'Spread your legs some.'

I kicked my stance wider and my husband – calm, cool and collected – drove a thick batch of fingers into me. Three, if I saw right. His thumb found my clit, his fingers my G-spot, and I chewed my bottom lip to keep from weeping.

Through it all, I touched the small silver lightning bolt at my throat.

He patted his lap. 'Come on.'

I followed his lead and held his offered hands while I straddled his lap. His hard cock nudged the split of my nether lips. All of me so wet with juices, the easy slide of his shaft along my clit made me freeze. I felt like I might come at any moment. Pain was dancing with pleasure and the result was a confused kind of urgent need.

'Raise up a little.'

I pressed my weight on my knees, raising my body so Chuck could rake his tip along my hole, and when he said, 'Lower,' I sank down on him one agonising inch at a time.

When he was fully seated in me, stretching me gorgeously, he said, 'Do. Not. Come.'

Eye to eye he waited for me to nod and I started to pray. *Please God, please don't let me come. Please don't …*

I lost my train of thought as he held the meaty part of my hips and rocked me, manipulating my motions so the pleasure built and built and built until I was nearly weeping with trying to restrain myself. With every motion, he drove up under me in short little bursts and, when I thought it was too much, I sobbed aloud and he *tsk*ed gently.

'OK, I'll take pity.' He sounded so reserved but his eyes were glazed and his jaw was tight. I was not the only one who was being tested.

He pulled free of me by pushing me back and the next order was issued. 'Over my knees.'

Oh fuck.

I sighed mightily, more from trying to get enough air than anything else. Slowly, I dropped to my knees and started to drape myself across him.

'Oh, before you do, take care of this,' Chuck said.

My lips on his soft fragrant skin – steeped in the musky scent of me and my arousal – I lapped at him. Licked him clean so his erection bobbed against my mouth. And when he told me, 'Enough,' I got my revenge by sucking him very hard one time in the way I knew always pushed him too close to the edge for comfort.

Chuck grabbed my long wavy hair and tugged me hard enough to bring tears to my eyes. 'I said enough.'

And then I was over his knee.

These are gentle. Don't worry ...

Problem was, gentle was worse than hard. Strokes one and two on my warm throbbing skin nearly made me come.

The thud rode through me and I felt the first tender flex of orgasm in my pussy.

Fuck.

'Count the rest for me, so I don't forget.'

'Three, four ...' I sighed.

He stopped to insert a finger into me. Chuck twisted it and pressed it and nudged it until silent tears rolled down my cheeks.

'My goodness, someone is tight.'

I didn't say anything. When the next blows fell, I whimpered, 'Five, six, seven ...'

This time he smoothed his hand up my spine, slowly trailing his fingertips up the ridges of my spine so all the fine hairs on me rose up and quivered.

'And the final ones.'

Tap-tap-tap.

He was barely striking me. It was just a mild vibration coursing through me, adding to the cacophony of arousal in my body. I pressed my thighs together and then realised that was stupid when I damn near orgasmed.

'Now go get us that nice bottle of wine.'

'I ... what?' I blinked and stood slowly. His hands on my arm and my spine as I rose, steadying me chivalrously.

'Go get us some wine. Take a little break before we go hard again.'

I took a deep breath to steel myself but as I turned he grabbed my wrist and tugged me back to stand right in front of him. 'Oh, I almost forgot.'

Chuck pressed his face to my pussy. He found my clit with the tip of his tongue, snaking it between my shaking legs to lap at me. He licked and licked and then sucked the hard knot of flesh.

All I could hear in my head was *don't come ... do not come ... don't come, Alice.* I heard it all the way up to the moment where I gripped his broad freckled shoulders and came. My pussy offering up a rush of fluid with every spasm.

Chuck calmly licked me clean and when his bright eyes found me he smiled. 'Uh-oh. Looks like someone is going to deserve every hard spank she gets. Now get the wine.'

He pinched my ass then, hard enough that my ears started to ring and my slick cunt grasped up around nothing again.

I hurried down to the kitchen on leaden feet. After finding glasses and a corkscrew, I paused to watch new snow falling. Just flurries and fluffs blowing in the wind. But pretty. And I imagined how it would feel to let that snow kiss the blushing flesh on my bottom. How cool it would feel when it melted on the pain-painted skin. How good.

I heard a creak upstairs and made my way back upstairs, legs shaking, flesh burning. 'Here we go,' I said softly.

Chuck had opened the blinds. Our bedroom sat high above other houses – this being an addition. So the only ones who had a view into our room despite the falling dusk were squirrels.

'Pretty, isn't it?'

I nodded, pouring out two glasses. My hand shook and the glasses tinkled together. Every heartbeat thundered in my cunt. Every cool drift of air spiked my nipples.

'Pretty like lightning but different.'

'Yes, different.'

Chuck patted the end of the bed and said, 'Sit.'

'I … um … it hurts.'

'Sit,' he said.

I sat. The feel of dropping so soon to that tender skin made me wince, but, God, how I wanted to come again. God, how I wanted him to fuck me.

'Tell me about it.' He sipped his wine watching the snow.

'You know this is the world's longest spanking!' I blurted. I tended to do that when frustrated and anxious.

Chuck smiled and patted my naked thigh. 'You know I never like to rush a good thing. Now tell me about it.'

'About what?'

'The lightning storm.'

'When we met?'

'Yes. Tell me about it again.'

I sipped my wine and felt the alcohol burn kiss my throat.

'It was my first day on campus and a violent storm rolled in. One of those that ushers out one season and ushers in the next. So summer was dying and fall was coming. And the wind whipped up and the sky turned pitch.'

'Like a movie about witches,' he said with a chuckle.

I nodded. We'd been saying that for ever, about the sky the day we met. 'Like a movie about witches – dark and foreboding and so low.'

'Like we could touch it.'

I nodded, silent.

'And?' he prodded, stroking my thigh all the way up to where it met my mound. A sudden jerk shot through me and I gasped. I was cold and I wanted to come and when he touched me I wanted to scream or laugh or cry.

Instead, I said, 'And lightning, white like snow and forked like the end of the world, split the sky and I hightailed it to that overhang by the Science building.'

'And?'

'And you were there,' I said, watching his hand. Watching it pet me. I parted my thighs just a bit and his fingers dipped into the middle but did not touch me where I wanted it most.

'And?'

'And you kissed me. You just ... kissed me. One moment the sky opened up and I was running. The next I hit shelter and you took one look at me, wet and dripping and ... kissed me.'

Chuck pushed his hand higher, holding it blunt like a knife. He nudged my clit with the edge of his hand before turning it to cup my mound. When his fingers invaded me, he whispered, lips pressed to my ear, 'You're wet and dripping now. Get up and stand against the wall. Press your body to it, Alice.'

So I set my wine down and obeyed.

I spread my body into an X and pressed myself to the

cool bedroom wall. I heard a sharp report and my heart thudded.

'Do you remember this?' he asked quietly.

I didn't have to look. I felt him run the thin balsam wood over my ass cheeks. Then up my back and across my shoulder so my entire body was at attention. I knew what it was – a decade-old paddle that had been a gag gift at my thirtieth birthday party. Ironic, considering I was about to hit another milestone, that it had rested untouched and snickered at only to be pulled out a decade later for use.

'Yes.'

'I think I'll use it. I could stand a little help. You really do have a firm little ass, Alice, and my hand is stinging like a motherfucker.'

I blinked at his vulgarity. So very much not Chuck, so it only ramped up my anticipation.

'This will hurt a bit, baby,' he said against the back of my neck.

The skin prickled and my pussy twitched and then my stomach had that free-falling feeling I remembered from earlier.

'Did you hear me?'

I nodded.

He smacked me with the paddle and the sharp sound hurt my ears. Fire bloomed along my skin and he said, 'Then answer me.'

'Yes, Chuck. I heard you.'

'Ass out.' Nipping my earlobe so a fresh trickle of fluid graced my nether lips, he waited for me to oblige. When I did, they rained down with a vengeance. No time for me to even count them off. But I did in my head. *Two ... three ... four ... five ...*

He stopped, running the thin sharp side of the paddle along my flanks so I twitched. It tickled and terrified and I found that I was panting as he touched me – even with a piece of wood.

'Why did I kiss you?'

He kissed the back of my neck, trailed the edge of his paddle between my legs from behind. The wood kissed my clitoris and I bucked as if he'd bitten my neck instead of dropping a hot little kiss.

'Because I was pretty.'

The paddle bumped me more snugly and I pressed my palms flat to the wall to focus.

'Wrong.'

'Because I was beautiful,' I amended.

'Good.'

Chuck stepped back and yanked my hips just so to jut my ass out and then I was swallowing hard to keep from crying. In my head I chanted. *Six ... seven ... eight ... nine ...*

The paddle hit the floor and the final blow was delivered with his hand. I sobbed aloud, the fire in my skin almost unbearable. Would I wear small black and blue freckles after this? Or possibly actual handprints? At any time I could have cried *uncle*. I could have asked him to stop and yet ... I didn't. I could already calculate multiple peeks at my purpling skin in the near future. My secret pleasure – looking, touching, prodding.

I pushed my ass back into his hand as the blow ended and Chuck lost his cool. He grunted, pushing me to the bed so that I rolled to my back. The tender skin he'd just abused screamed but, when he thrust my legs high, so high they crushed my breasts to my chest, pushing the air out of me, I followed readily. I followed eagerly. I wanted him in me and he drove in with a small desperate sound and a look almost akin to anger in his eyes.

'Jesus, fuck,' he rasped. 'You are so wet.'

'I know.'

'And tight.'

'I know.' My fingers clutched and plucked at him, eager to touch him everywhere – anywhere.

'And beautiful.'

I blushed.

'And I love you.'

'I know. And I love you.'

That was that, the talk was done. Big hands pressing my knees high, splaying me, opening me for him. Chuck drove into me. His gaze stayed trained on where we joined and he slowed. Watching eagerly every inch of himself disappear into my body until I whispered, 'Please, baby. Please.'

Then he crushed his body over mine, rocking his hips; the bump and grind of his pelvis to my clit would get me off. He knew this was how I liked it and he was going to take me there. He rolled his pelvis, getting deeper with every motion, and when I couldn't stand it anymore I let myself go. The pleasure burst up and out of me when I came, crying out his name. Chuck pushed his mouth to mine, licked the nonsense words from my lips and tilted my hips up just a bit more. With his strong hands under my stinging bottom, I came again.

'You didn't ... there's still ...' I was shaking my head. My entire body fatigued and rejuvenated at the same time.

'I know. I know. Roll over,' he said, laughing as he pushed me on to my belly. Yanking me up on hands and knees, he skittered his fingers over every weal and welt. Over every singing bit of flesh and every twitching inch of muscle.

He entered me from behind, one hand on the small of my back, one hand travelling over my ass. And as he thrust he gently tapped. Counting.

'One for Alice. Two for Alice. Three for Alice. Four.'

His thumb slid along my soaked slit and then he pressed it into my ass. The pressure and the pain adding to the mélange of sensations, making me whimper.

'Five for Alice. Six for Alice. Seven for Alice ... eight.'

His voice had gone gritty and raw. He was panting as

54

he fucked me, each light tap on my skin earmarking a deep thrust into my cunt.

We both froze and he said, 'Touch yourself, baby.' His voice was thick and needful.

He was so close. And that just made my entire body ready. A thrill shot through the centre of me, a burst of bliss in my brain that rocketed through my core, hitting my belly and then lower, as I pushed my fingers to my clit and started to manipulate myself.

I could feel heat in my cheeks – both sets – and, when Chuck's movements resumed, I had to bite my tongue to sharpen my mind.

'Nine, I love you. Ten ... I love you.' He roared and gave me one last gentle spank and shuddered behind me. 'And one to grow on.'

The feel of him coming undone buckled me. I came as my body went down, crying out his name. The pain of my spanking an achy dull thud, the thrill of it fresh and vibrant through all of me.

He pulled me in and kissed my head, my cheek, my brow. When he kissed my lips, I turned and pressed myself to him, crushing my mouth to his, sucking his tongue. My hand found his cock damp and warm.

'How was that?'

'You tell me how it was,' I teased.

'It was ... wow.'

'Oh, now you're at a loss for words,' I snorted.

He pulled me closer, pinching a nipple so I gasped. When he stroked my bottom gently, I winced.

'Did I overdo it?'

'No.'

'Did you ... *like* it?' He chuckled.

'What do you think?'

Small warm blips of pleasure coursed through my body, and I shifted closer to wrap my leg around him. Outside the sky had turned to slate, the snow illuminated by a nearby streetlamp.

'I think yes.'

'I think you're right.'

'So about the rest of the stuff on your list,' he started.

'Yes?' My fingers returned to the lightning bolt charm. Now it would remind me not only of when we met, but also of this. This enormous new thing in our lives.

'Promise me you won't buy anything else on it.' He stared me down, his warm brown eyes full of humour and affection.

I paused as if I were considering. 'You know ... about that ...' I kissed his shoulder and then his pecs.

'Yes, darling?' He smirked, waiting.

My head was full of what we'd just done. The sound of the blows in my ears, his hands on me, the pain that sparked and flared into pleasure ... the orgasms.

'Yeah ... I can't make you any promises on that, honey.'

Black, White and Red All Over
Lolita Lopez

I trembled with anxiety and excitement as I waited for Derek to return. The unforgiving wooden planks beneath my knees offered little comfort to my aching joints. Beads of sweat travelled the naked curves of my body. Breasts pushed forward, back arched, hands gripping my ankles, I was contorted in the worst way but didn't dare move.

Derek seemed to have a sixth sense for that sort of thing. He'd walk in here, take one look at me, and immediately know I'd straightened my back to ease the pressure or rolled my shoulders. And he'd be so disappointed. I strove to make him proud, to please him in every way during our sessions. I closed my eyes and tried to ignore the twinge in my side and the awful burn along my neck. My reward would come soon enough.

I'd lost track of how long I'd been waiting in that tense position. Twenty minutes? Thirty? I couldn't say. Derek always kept me on my toes. Some weeks, we'd get right to business. Other times, he'd make me wait, draw out the anticipation and dread as long as possible. He seemed to enjoy my reactions the most when he put me through my paces with stress positions and other little torturous delights.

My ears perked to the sound of footsteps approaching Derek's office. I fought the urge to lift my head and glance towards the door. I imagined Derek looming in the doorway, his dark skin so beautiful against the stark whiteness of the crisp dress shirts he preferred. No tie, of course. He'd have tossed that aside with his cufflinks and jacket while I was kneeling there on the floor of his office.

Belly wobbling with anticipation, I listened intently to the heavy footfalls drawing closer. His smell swirled around me. Those pleasing notes of cedar and sandalwood infiltrated my system and saturated my lungs. God, I'd missed his smell so much over the last week. I'd taken to spritzing my pillow with his cologne and hugging it tightly as I played with my pussy and climaxed again and again. I'd pretended it was his tongue circling my clit instead of my fingers. I hated his business trips, hated the way they took him away from me and left me alone in this big old house of his.

But he was back now, and I was going to get exactly what I deserved.

Derek circled me, his harsh gaze taking in the odd angles of my bent body. I kept my gaze fixed on the wooden beams running the length of the ceiling. I didn't dare break the protocol he'd enacted when he'd sent me into the office. I so desperately wanted to show him that I could follow the rules and exceed his expectations. It had taken me so fucking long to find the right dominant, to find my Derek, to find a man strong enough to fulfil all my needs. I'd do whatever it took to keep him.

Derek stopped behind me. 'Sit up straight. Eyes down.'

'Yes, sir.' I instantly followed his directions. The discomfort eased as I readjusted my strained body to a more natural pose. He was such a good dominant. He never kept me in an awkward position too long or tied me up too tightly. I was never even tempted to use our safe word. I trusted him implicitly and knew he'd keep me safe.

'I'm very unhappy with this report, Hallie.' He flicked the paper I'd handed him when he'd walked in the door an hour earlier. 'Skipped breakfast one morning. Missed two workouts. Cancelled the pampering session I booked for you at the spa so you could stay late at work.' He clicked his teeth. 'What am I going to do with you?'

'Punish me, sir?' *Oh, please, please, please*, I silently begged.

59

The paper fluttered to the floor next to my bare foot. Derek bent forward and palmed my small breast. He'd so carefully rolled up the sleeves of his shirt. Every fold was precise and clean and revealed inch after inch of his well-defined forearms.

I loved the way his dark skin looked against mine. We made such a striking couple. Where I was petite and pale and blonde, Derek stood six feet five and had the most beautiful brown skin and buzzed black hair. We were a mismatched pair in looks but in the bedroom, office and playroom we were perfectly paired.

'You have been a very bad, bad girl.' Derek pinched my pebbled nipple between his thick fingers, and I gasped. 'But maybe you deliberately broke my rules, Hallie. Perhaps I should just send you to bed right now.'

Fear clutched my chest. 'Oh, no, sir! Please, sir. I need to be punished. I need to learn my lesson.'

'You want to be punished?' Derek squeezed my nipple even harder and made me whine. 'You want me to bend you over that desk and paddle your backside?'

'Oh, yes. Yes!' I shook with excitement at the very thought of the flat red paddle cracking against my ass and making me jump with every whack. 'Please, sir. Please.'

Derek chuckled and released my breast. 'We'll see.'

I panted as he walked away from me. My heart clamoured in my chest, and I ached for his touch. My gaze stayed on the floor, but I listened carefully as he moved around the room. The armless wooden chair that sat behind his desk scraped and squealed as he dragged it to an open spot. He plunked it down hard and sat down, the soft rustling of his trousers filling in the blanks for me.

'Hallie? Eyes up.' He patted his lap when I gazed at him. 'Come here, little one.'

I fought the urge to scamper over like a hyperactive puppy. Instead, I leaned forward and dropped to all fours. I pretended to be a sleek jungle cat as I crawled towards him, my hips swinging seductively and my movements long and smooth. I knelt at his side and pressed my cheek to his thigh.

Derek hummed in appreciation and caressed my face. 'Well done, sweetheart. Now, climb up here.'

I rose slowly and draped myself across his wide lap. The welcoming heat of his body relaxed my raw nerves. I breathed in his scent as I placed my fingertips on the floor and let my toes lift from the ground. The chair was just tall enough to keep me off balance. I think Derek deliberately chose it for that attribute. He seemed to enjoy keeping me off-kilter and uncertain.

Derek's hand stroked my spine, and I shivered. He swept aside my hair so that it fell over my shoulder and hid most of my face. With my back clear, he resumed his gentle petting. His fingers drifted along the cleft between my cheeks. Up and down and side to side. I clenched my buttocks and wished his fingers would move even lower and brush against my clit. The needy little nub craved attention.

I gasped with shock as Derek's flat palm cracked against my ass. 'Ow!'

'Quiet.' He smacked my bottom four more times in rapid succession, his palm jumping from cheek to cheek. I quickly realised there was no way to anticipate when or where or how hard he would spank me again. His hand alternated from slow to fast whacks and hard to soft blows. Over and over again, his big hand beat my ass.

I wiggled and cried out with each smack. Pain blossomed under his palm. My skin prickled, and I tried to inch away and escape the blows. It was folly. Every time I moved, the forearm clamped just below my shoulders pressed down even harder. My ass was on fire, but Derek wasn't about to let up. I knew him too well. The first two dozen or so smacks were just the warm-up. I was really going to get it now.

And it thrilled me. Frissons of deliciously dirty excitement rippled through my belly. Slick juices flooded my clenching cunt. My clit throbbed, and I used the momentum of every spank to press my mound against his leg. I felt like a naughty little poodle humping his thigh, but it just felt so damn good. The burst of stinging pain from his cracking palm accentuated the lovely tingle around my clit when I rubbed against him.

'Hold still.'

'I can't! It *hurts*.'

'You will hold still.' Derek's gruff voice didn't have the effect he'd intended. I couldn't stop. That pink pearl controlled my thoughts, and he knew it. Derek reached down and took hold of my arms. He secured my wrists at the small of my back. I tried to pull free but his big paw held my wrists in place. 'Quit squirming.'

'Yes, sir!' A loud crack echoed in the room as Derek went to town on my backside. I cried out but held still as he delivered my punishment. Left, right, right, right, left, left, left. There was no rhythm or pattern to his spankings. He'd mastered the art of a good ass-whooping better than any dominant I'd ever had the pleasure of playing with, and he knew it.

Derek whispered softly as his palm connected with my ass over and over. 'So pretty and pink.' He spanked my left cheek three times and then landed a fourth whack to my right side. 'Oh, honey, you should see my big handprint on your sweet ass.'

I was sobbing now. The pain and blazing heat were too much. I pressed against his thigh again. The wicked friction of his leg against my clit eased the hurt. Quivers of lust tickled my core. I shuddered as Derek abandoned my spanking and brushed his warm hand over the curve of my battered behind. His fingers travelled the length of my crack and dipped even lower. I sucked in a sharp breath as he got dangerously close to my clit.

'You're so wet, Hallie.' His fingers played in the silky nectar seeping from my pussy. I heard him sucking on his fingertips and nearly came right then. 'Mmmm. So good.'

'Please, sir.' I clenched my thighs together. 'Please.'

'Do you want to come, Hallie?' His fingers probed my wet cunt. 'Is that what you want?'

'Oh, yes, sir.' I pushed back against his searching fingers. 'Please.'

'Maybe,' he said in that uncertain tone of his. 'You were a very naughty girl.'

Even as he considered denying me the orgasm I so desperately needed, Derek found my clit and circled the hot button with his fingertips. I opened my thighs as wide as possible, granting him as much access as he desired, and groaned loudly. Pleasure coiled low and tight inside me. It wouldn't take much to send me reeling into climax. I wanted to climax so badly, so badly.

'Do you want to come, baby girl?'

'Yes, sir.' I was openly weeping now. 'I want to come. Want to come all over your fingers.'

'All over my fingers?' He strummed my clit even faster. 'Would you soak my hand?'

'Yes, sir. Oh, yes.' I flexed my legs and tried to squeeze every ounce of stimulation from his skilful fingers.

The Delights of Spanking

'I bet you would,' he said with a little laugh. 'But,' he sighed, 'no, Hallie.' He spoke with such finality it stunned me. He abruptly removed his fingers from me and left me gasping and jerking across his lap. 'Not tonight, Hallie.'

In the haze of lust, I spoke without thinking. 'Yes, tonight. I want it now. Touch me, Derek. Make me come.'

He scoffed and let out a guffaw. 'I'm sorry. Have we forgotten how this works? *I* tell *you* what to do, Hallie. Not the other way around.'

Before I could apologise for my outburst, Derek quickly stood, lifted me from his lap and spun me around to face his desk. He placed his hand between my shoulder blades and pushed my breasts flat against the desktop. I inhaled a nervous breath as I heard the top drawer on the left open. Would it be the cane, the paddle or the strap?

Please be the paddle. Oh, God, please, please, please.

My heart stuttered as I heard the dreaded snap of the strap as Derek tested it between his hands. I vibrated with a mix of fear and excitement. I hated that strap more than any other implement Derek possessed, but it also pushed me into that ethereal plane of subspace faster than anything else in his arsenal.

'Palms flat on the desk, Hallie.' His warm hand caressed my lower back as he delivered his stern directions. That was the core of our relationship. Strict but

65

gentle. Loving but injurious. Controlling yet freeing. We were the definition of mind-fuck but we did it so very well. 'You *will* use your safe word if it's too much.'

I didn't get a chance to do more than nod before the kiss of the leather strap knocked the air from my lungs. The leather was cold against my hot skin but the sting was so impossibly sharp. I howled as Derek applied the strap with such finesse to my poor, abused bottom. The staccato slap echoed in the room and mixed with my cries and sobs.

Trembling and shaking, I tried to figure out where the pain ended and the pleasure began. The nerve-endings throughout my plump cheeks misfired. One second I felt the prickling bite of the strap and the next only the soothing burn of its painful kiss. My body responded so peculiarly. This was the pleasure part of the agony that I craved so deeply.

And this was why I loved Derek to the very depths of my soul. Only he understood what I wanted and needed to function. Every fibre of my being required this kind of ecstasy and torment. Derek gave me exactly what I needed without ever having to ask. He possessed an innate and uncanny ability to apply just the right amount of punishment to make me feel complete. We seemed to be matched on a sub-atomic level. Surely, it was fate that two halves had finally connected.

I was vaguely aware of the strap hitting the floor. Behind

me, Derek unzipped his pants. A thick muscled forearm slid around my chest and hauled me up off the desk. His long fingers cupped my cheek and turned my face towards his. He claimed my mouth in a passionate kiss that made my toes curl. The taste of mint and sugary sweetness exploded on my taste buds. He groaned hungrily as he devoured my mouth.

'God, I missed you, Hallie.' He squeezed my breast and brushed his thumb across the stiff nipple. 'I wanted you so badly.'

'Take me,' I begged, my pussy so wet the insides of my thighs were slick. I pushed back against him, not minding the God-awful scrape of his open zipper on my tender skin. 'Fuck me, Derek.'

He forced my legs wide by pressing the toe of his shoe against my ankles. He reached between our bodies and lined up his fat cock with my entrance. With one rough thrust, he slid home. My eyes widened at the sudden intrusion. 'Oh!'

'Did you miss my cock, Hallie?' He pulled out until just the crown of his impressive dick remained buried inside me and then plunged deep again. 'Did you?'

'Yes!' My feet lifted from the ground, and I slapped at the desk as he fucked me with abandon. His strong arm braced my waist and bore most of my weight, freeing my body to accept his jackhammering cock without problem. He was just so big inside of me. My pussy still resisted him a little. The stretch and slight burn ramped up my pleasure. 'More, Derek. Harder. Oh, God, *harder*.'

Lips dancing along my shoulder and neck, Derek delivered exactly what I wanted. He urged me on with softly spoken words. 'Do you know how beautiful you are to me? Do you have any idea what you do to me, woman?' He nipped a sensitive patch along the curve of my neck. 'You make me crazy, Hallie.'

My fingers squelched against the shiny surface of the desk. I closed my eyes and enjoyed the rich timbre of his voice. My breasts jiggled every time he pounded my pussy. They were so heavy and ached with the need to be touched. I let one of my hands leave the desk and move to my breast. I rolled my nipple between my fingertips. The needy peak grew hard. Electric zings arced through my chest.

'That's it, baby. Play with your nipples.' Derek's tongue swirled along my neck before he sucked hard enough to leave a love bite. The pulling sensation seemed to travel right to my clit. I was reminded of how skilfully Derek ate pussy. The man could reduce me to a quivering, boneless mass in less than six minutes.

I groaned as Derek's cock slipped in and out of my juicy cunt like a well-oiled piston. He had amazing stamina and speed. I loved the way he drove so deep inside me. There was a time and place for slow and gentle, but it wasn't here. Tonight, we were making up for lost time. We were nearly frantic in our coupling, as if we feared this was simply another tormenting dream, and we'd soon wake to discover we were alone in our beds for yet another night.

When Derek's fingers discovered my clit, I nearly screamed. 'Make me come, Derek. I want to come all over your cock.'

Behind me, Derek growled. He loved it when I talked dirty. He'd never admit it, but I think he secretly enjoyed when I pushed the established boundaries of our relationship. I was the submissive, but that didn't mean that I didn't want to exert a little control here and there. Besides, every time I pushed him, he pushed back with a punishment. In the end, we both got exactly what we wanted.

He snapped his hips and drover deeper inside my pussy. I couldn't get enough and wanted more, more, more of him. Those fingers circling my clit found the perfect rhythm. That coiled spring of pleasure so tight and low in my belly suddenly burst free. Spasms of pleasure wracked my body. I was coming and coming and coming. Ass on fire, pussy fluttering, I surfed the waves of my orgasm. 'Derek. Derek. Derek!'

'Oh, Hallie.' His voice had deepened, and I knew he was close. I rocked back against him, wanting to squeeze every ounce of pleasure from his steely shaft. 'God. *God!*'

Derek slammed balls-deep in my pussy and roared as he shot hot jets of come. He jerked and shuddered as his cock twitched until every last drop of semen had emptied inside me. With a loud groan, Derek slumped forward and pressed his cheek to my shoulder. I loved the feeling of his weight on top of me, pushing me down, and reached back to caress his waist. Derek's mouth ghosted across my shoulder. 'I love you so much, Hallie.'

A sappy grin curved my lips. Derek was always so honest and romantic after our trysts. Normally it was like pulling teeth to get an admission of love from him, but one little mind-blowing orgasm and he was suddenly Cyrano whispering sweet nothings.

'I love you, too.'

He made a happy sound that wasn't quite a chuckle before he pulled out of me. I felt so empty without him but I didn't have to worry. Always the good dominant, Derek scooped me up and cradled me to his chest. He carried me over to the chair where he'd soundly whipped my ass and held me tight. Our fluids mingled and made a mess of his trousers but he didn't seem to care. We were both blissed out of our minds and silly thoughts of dry cleaning didn't even register.

'You know,' Derek said finally, 'I didn't want to tell you earlier, but I have another trip scheduled at the end of the month.'

I pouted up at him. 'You said no more trips for the rest of the year.'

'I know.' He looked upset about breaking his promise.

'This is something that can't be put off until the New Year. It's best to deal with it before December begins. But,' he said brightly and stroked my cheek, 'think of it this way: if you break rules the same way you did during this trip, you'll earn yourself one hell of a spanking session.'

There was no mistaking the amusement in his voice or the perverted grin he sported. That would be just like him to look forward to tanning my backside with that dastardly strap of his.

I started to reply, but he put a finger to my lips. 'Don't even try to convince me those skipped breakfasts and workouts weren't on purpose. I know you too well, Hallie.'

'Yeah, well,' I grumbled as I toyed with the buttons on his shirt. 'I missed you. I missed this.' I gestured around the office. 'You know how I am.'

'Oh, I know all right.' He kissed me until I was breathless and mewling like a kitten. 'And I know you really want me to pick you up and carry you into the bathroom for a hot shower and a massage.'

I decided to go for broke. 'And maybe another round of hot sex.'

Derek narrowed his eyes. 'Well, you have been a very good girl tonight.'

I happily nodded and slipped back into my submissive role. 'Oh, yes, sir.'

'And that sweet little ass of yours is the prettiest shade of red I've seen in a long time.' His fingers trailed the curve of my sore bottom. 'I suppose you've earned a nice reward.'

I grinned and nuzzled my nose against his. 'Reward me, sir.'

Derek laughed and rose from the chair, my weight easily shifted by his big strong arms. He pecked my forehead as he carted me out of the office, pausing just long enough for me to reach out and flip the light switch. I snuggled close to his familiar warmth and let my eyes close.

There weren't many girls out there who would enjoy a Friday night shut-in with a boyfriend who had a dirty little penchant for the darker side of hands-on attention. The way I figured it, this night could only get better and better. This was my heaven, my dream date, and I couldn't wait to experience whatever Derek had in store for me next.

Retro
Teresa Noelle Roberts

I did my best never to imagine Darren, my swing dance partner, as a potential life partner. It still happened, of course, but I squelched those fancies as soon as they started.

A playmate was another story. I wasted a lot of time fantasising about all the sexy mischief he and I might get up to in some alternative universe where a meaningless but hot fling wouldn't ruin our friendship. But a partner? That way lay madness.

He was just too good-looking and dapper, with his cool retro clothes, his fedora, his rich brown skin and high cheekbones, to be a good fit for me. I'm pretty, sexy even, in a low-maintenance way, but elegant or stylish, not so much. Much as I like forties and fifties clothing,

I end up in jeans and hoodies unless it's a special occasion. Darren was polished, with a sense of style I envied; even when he wasn't 'dressed up', he managed to look sharp. To make it even more frustrating from my point of view, he had a model's striking face, but he wasn't model-perfect – he had an attractively blocky build, not some lean, sculpted designer dream-body – which meant he was in my attractive-but-not-oh-my-gawd league, not in line to date starlets or Kardashians. And he was just plain fun, sharing my love for vintage films, retro cocktails, and jazz and swing music. If he'd been gay, he'd have been my perfect BFF.

Can you imagine being disappointed that a sexy, smart guy who shared your interests *wasn't* gay? I know it sounds odd, but a case of the hopeless hots for someone I could never get would be easier to handle than one for someone who was theoretically attainable, just a bad idea.

Darren was gorgeous but that was only the start of why I lusted after him. The way he could guide me about a dance floor, controlling my movements with the lightest, most sensitive touch, as if we shared one mind – or as if I'd surrendered my will over to him and all I had to do was follow his lead – was meltingly sexy and made me want to surrender myself to him, right there as we danced. I didn't just want to fuck him, or even simply date him. I wanted to be his happy submissive, following his will in the bedroom and out, as I did on the dance floor, getting spanked when I was bad and spanked with a different attitude when I was good. I was an old-fashioned girl at heart, albeit an old-fashioned girl with a few twists, and I wanted a man who'd be in charge in the relationship: not just kinky sex, but actual domination and submission and the occasional domestic discipline. As I'd gotten to know Darren better, I realised I wanted him to be that man.

The problem was, I suspected that, if I made that particular offer, Darren would run in horror.

He was so unfailingly polite. His parents had definitely raised him right, in a way that fit his retro look. He called people older than him 'sir' and 'ma'am', and opened the door for women even though we teased him about it. When Nedra did the fundraiser for the domestic-violence hotline, he was the first person in the group to whip out his wallet, muttering something about how real men knew better than to raise a hand against a woman.

Which I utterly agreed with, in the context Nedra was talking about. The way he put it, though, I just couldn't see Darren being into spanking, let alone a relationship that involved spanking and domination and discipline as a serious component. That meant we weren't likely to be suited long term. The best possible result would be an amazing fling that might make things awkward between us afterwards.

Hence occasionally wishing he were gay. It would be safer and less frustrating. Hell, I could tell Theoretical Gay Darren about my politically incorrect yearnings for some other theoretical dude and he'd not only sympathise, he might even counter with an amusingly scandalous yarn about some kinky experience he'd had. But the real Darren? No way.

At least I thought so until Darren invited a few of us over for a night of vintage movies and retro cocktails. We'd already watched *The Philadelphia Story*, swooning over the clothes, and were part-way through *It Happened One Night*. Darren, busy playing host, had been nursing a single old-school dry martini all night long, but the rest of us had been sampling brandy Alexanders, Manhattans, sidecars, and other concoctions swilled by our grandparents with more *Thin Man* abandon than common sense.

So, when Clark Gable smacked the beautiful, bratty Claudette Colbert, we all reacted in a completely unvarnished way. Nedra rose unsteadily to her feet and tried to stalk out in protest. Instead, she swayed for a few seconds, realised her girlfriend Heather, who didn't drink, had the car keys and wasn't budging off the couch, and sank down again, muttering something under her breath about abusive patriarchal paradigms. Jenny, in perfect tipsy-grad-student fashion, began declaiming, 'It's from the thirties. You have to see it in historical context, in relation to their class differences ...'

Heather, probably noticing that several of us were poised to throw things at both of them to stop the pontification, suggested they take the discussion into the kitchen.

And in the ensuing silence, I admitted, before I could self-censor, 'I think it's hot.'

Nedra shot daggers at me.

Undeterred – the Manhattan I'd just finished was clearly doing the driving – I expounded on my theory. 'Well, isn't it? He's all tough and thuggy and she's pretty and spoiled, and you know they're into each other but can't say it so this is how they're expressing it. She acts bratty, he takes charge. A real spanking would have been sexier, but maybe the actress wouldn't do that.'

Everyone stared. A few people conceded that, in the context of the movie, she probably had been asking for it and it probably was meant to be titillating – but no one agreed that it was. Things might have gotten even weirder, except the buzzer went off and we put the movie on pause so Lee could get his famous homemade pizza out of the oven. By the time we got back to the film, my outburst was lost in the distraction of four cheeses and sausage.

By everyone but me.

Even nearly perfect pizza couldn't distract me from the images that had risen in my mind, from the hopeless fantasy that Darren would someday take charge of me that way. OK, not exactly that way, but instead giving me a good sound spanking when I deserved it. I barely saw the rest of the movie. Instead, I stared at Darren's dark, deft hands and imagined them pulling me down over his strong thighs and smacking down on to my butt while he instructed me in better behaviour.

Darren was a responsible host. Not long after the pizza came out, he pronounced last call at the bar. The movie wound to its happy ending as we nibbled and let the booze leave our systems. Mostly sobered up by the time the credits rolled, I managed not to express the theory that if the heroine hadn't enjoyed the hero's high-handed treatment, or at least enjoyed making up afterwards, there wouldn't have been a happy ending. The character was ditzy and naive, but she wasn't dumb, and she had a good grasp on her own best interests.

I knew I'd fall for a guy who'd call me on my b.s. and punish me for it if necessary, but the dom of my dreams was dark-skinned and elegant, not white and scruffy, like Clark Gable's character in the film.

Yeah, dream on.

I'd taken the bus over, knowing there would be cocktails, but, as I picked up my coat, Darren put his hand on my arm. 'A guy got mugged at the bus stop the other night. I'll give you a ride once everyone's gone.'

He didn't phrase it like a question.

As my dance partner, Darren had touched me many

78

times, but his hand on my arm reverberated through me. It was a little tighter than it needed to be, almost possessive, matching his tone of voice. At least my imagination told me that, although I couldn't hope it was true.

'Uh, sure.' I thought I'd sobered up, but, as soon as Darren touched me, my brain fogged and I felt just as giddy as I had on my third Manhattan. 'But you don't need to go to so much trouble for me.' I was delighted by the offer, but it was late and I didn't want to be a pest.

'Gina, there's a mugger in the neighbourhood. You're not waiting for the bus alone.'

Suddenly and stupidly, I felt compelled to argue. There was just enough bourbon in my body to decide that he was being overprotective, condescending. On the other hand, it had been a while – as in since I stopped living with my dad – since a man worried enough about me to get annoyingly overprotective, and it felt pretty damn good, so I was mostly arguing on principle. 'I bet you'd let Lee take the bus.'

'Lee's six four and looks like a Marine. Probably no one's going to mess with him. I'd still offer him a ride but I wouldn't push it if he said no.'

He implied that he'd push it if I said no. That he'd make the decision for me.

What a jerk, half of me said. Some caveman gene had woken up from a long sleep tonight.

Dominant and protective, the other half of me said. I might not need to be protected or even want it, but I had a few Neanderthal genes of my own and they made both my heart and my panties melt.

The last few guests came up to offer thanks and hugs goodbye, so I didn't argue. Inwardly, though, I was sputtering as I said goodnight to our friends.

Sputtering and getting wet, especially since I noticed Darren only moved his hand off my arm when he had to accept a hearty, back-slapping hug from Lee.

When everyone was gone, though, I just had to open my big mouth. Maybe it was my pride as a woman of the 2010s speaking, or maybe, just maybe, it was memories of tonight's movie, *Kiss Me Kate* and several old Westerns involving the feisty Maureen O'Hara getting her comeuppance from John Wayne after – at least in the eyes of a spanko like me – setting herself up for it. 'I'm a big girl, Daddy. I can take the bus.' I paused mischievously as Darren's mouth set into a line that might have been annoyance, suppressed laughter or an unholy combination of pissed off and amused. 'Oops. You're not my dad. My dad's in Chicago and, guess what, he started letting me go out at night fifteen years ago. Back off.'

Instead of backing off, though, Darren stepped even closer, so we were all but touching again. He wasn't a huge guy, not like Lee, but he was still bigger than me and he was getting that I've-had-enough look on his face that Gable gave to Colbert just before things got interesting. His eyes held a glint of mischief, and a hint of something else, something that made his pupils widen and turned his brown eyes the colour of bourbon backlit by fire. 'Do you really want me to back off?' he asked. 'I was hoping you wanted me to get closer.'

Was he saying that? Was he *really* saying that?

It took my shocked brain a few seconds to put together the words, the look in his eyes, the half-smile breaking out over the pseudo-sternness, even the sudden protectiveness. I nodded slowly, speechless at hearing words I'd barely let myself daydream.

He pulled me close and whispered, 'I picked that movie for a reason, although I'd remembered the scene as a spanking, not just one smack to get her attention. I was hoping to get a clue how you'd react to that sort of thing.' He laughed, and it set my bones on fire. 'I didn't expect you to make it quite as clear as you did.'

Suddenly I couldn't meet his eyes. 'You mix a strong drink,' I mumbled, 'or I might have been more subtle.'

'And you had three, which is more than you should have.'

Half my instincts told me to protest at the 'should have', except the other half of my instincts– the old-fashioned, submissive half– assured me a) he was right; I should have stopped at the second and maybe asked

81

for the second one to be small; and b) I really, really liked that he cared enough to be stern with me, especially since he was saying stern things, but smiling sexily as he did.

'Would have been smarter,' I admitted, 'but they were so tasty.'

He shook his head. 'No self-control ... but we can work on that together, if you agree. On the other hand, if you hadn't enjoyed the drinks so much, I might still be wondering whether you might be interested in a relationship that was a little old-fashioned and a little kinky, kind of *Father Knows Best* with spanking and a better soundtrack.'

My heart did funny fluttery things. So did my pussy. I could hardly believe what I was hearing. There were so many things I wanted to say, but the words all caught in my throat. I looked away again, embarrassed by what must be showing on my face: confusion, eagerness, gratitude and naked need.

He touched the side of my face. 'Gina?'

I worked my way to a clear thought, though it wasn't as well put as I might have liked. 'The only thing I'd like better, Darren, is very old-fashioned and very kinky.' I paused. 'I think, anyway.' Then the words started pouring out. 'I love spanking, but I also want someone to take charge and keep me in line when I'm bad, not only play for fun. I think. I've never done anything like that outside the bedroom before.

Something about you in your retro clothes made me start daydreaming about it, but I felt dirty because you're such a good guy. But now I know you're into it too, I feel dirty in a good way. Did any of that make sense?'

Darren drew me in for a kiss that told me he'd understood me whether I'd made sense or not. He wound one hand through my hair like he was scruffing a kitten and I went boneless as a kitten would. I knew he had muscles from leaning against him in the course of dancing, but now Darren's strength surrounded me, supported me at the same time as it overwhelmed my senses. His lips and tongue were soft – he wasn't a ravaging kisser, at least not this first time – but he explored my mouth more thoroughly than it had ever been before. It felt possessive, like he was getting to know his newly claimed territory, but tender as well. I'd known he cared about me as a friend, but this kiss assured me he wasn't seeing me as just a friend with kinky benefits, but something more, as I'd hoped he could be something more. It was a kiss that drenched my panties and stiffened my nipples to the point that my lacy bra became an instrument of delicious torture – but it was also a kiss that promised many more kisses to come, some of them wilder and fiercer than this one and some of them soft kisses before sleep.

When we finally ended the kiss, I was trembling with desire and consumed by curiosity. 'Where do we go from here?' I asked.

Darren was still holding me so close I could feel the chuckle coming before I heard it. 'We talk, a lot. We have similar fantasies but we need to make sure we're on the same page about how to make them work in real life.'

I suppressed the urge to exclaim, 'Duh!' I suppose, if communicating was all that obvious, people (and I don't just mean kinky people) wouldn't get into relationships without having a clue what the other person really wanted. 'How about I ask the question I meant to ask instead of the one I did – what did you have in mind in the next couple of hours? I know we have a lot to talk about, but we also have a lot of previously unrequited lusting to get out of our systems.' I wriggled against him to get my point across. 'I'm sure we could figure out a few things without too much negotiation, such as spanking seems to be on both our minds right now ...'

I couldn't decide if his answering smile should be called a grin or a smirk. It was broad and delighted and just a little smug. 'I've been dying to spank your ass since the first time I saw you bending over. You have a very spankable ass, you know that?' He thwacked me once to prove his point.

I don't know about my ass being especially spankable, but it's especially appreciative of spanking. The way I first ground against him, then stuck my butt out for more, probably got that point across.

'Oh yes!' Darren guided me over to the couch, gesturing for me to sit beside him, 'a nice long sensual spanking, followed by me exploring every bit of your body until you scream and beg me to take you ... that sounds like a good start.'

His voice, I swear, dropped an octave when he talked dirty, and he was a baritone to start with. I shivered with need and delight. 'Yum. Do I get to explore you at the same time?'

His breath caught in his throat. 'If you do too much exploring, I might not be able to take my time.' He paused. 'Although fast and hard has its merits. Don't you agree?'

Damn, except for the one amazing kiss and the one thwack on my ass, we'd mostly been talking. If my nipples could have whimpered for Darren's hand and mouth on them, they would have. If my pussy could have been begged for his cock, it would have. What my butt would plead for would make most people sputter and blush. But his voice, and his attention, was arousing me as much as a direct touch from someone else might. Something I'd long desired was coming to fruition, and so much more wonderfully than even my fertile imagination had pictured, since Darren apparently dreamed of the same style of relationship I did.

'Maybe hard and fast would be best tonight and we can try for slow and sensual next time?' I sounded almost too eager, even to my own ears.

But damn it, I *was* eager!

Darren kissed me very gently, then said, 'Let me make that decision, Gina. Control is important to me. Controlling myself. Controlling you, as much as you'll let me.'

'As much as you'd like,' I blurted, aware that my libido rather than my brain was talking.

He put his finger across my lips. 'That sounds perfect to me, which is why we're going to have that long talk later, not now. Right now we're both too worked up to think, and I think we'll be that way until we've worn each other out at least once. But there's one thing we're doing tonight that *will* be hard and fast.' He grasped my wrists. 'You weren't exactly well behaved tonight. Drinking too much. Saying things that embarrassed half our friends and made the others wonder what freaky stuff you're into. Being belligerent and bratty when I told you I'd give you a ride rather than let you meet the local mugger. You've earned yourself a good hard spanking before we get to the tender stuff. This one will hurt.'

I gasped. My brain fogged. And my nipples and pussy informed me they'd liked his authoritative tone a lot.

'Panties off,' he ordered, and I obeyed, turned on by the deep delicious rumble of his voice and even more turned on by my own obedience. I slithered my black lace-trimmed tanga off from under my dress. I kicked my shoes off to get rid of the by-now drenched panties, but complied when he said, 'Put the shoes back on, please. I like them.'

For the party – OK, for Darren – I'd upgraded my usual jeans and flats to a flirty deep-green cocktail dress that looked vintage with its fitted bodice and full skirt, but wasn't, and black peep-toe high-heeled pumps. At the moment, I wasn't sure if dressing like this was the best idea I'd ever had or the worst, when I found myself upended over Darren's lap, skirt flipped up, high-heeled feet flailing a bit.

'Hard and fast,' he murmured. 'I like that you're independent and cheeky – it's part of what makes you fun – but I value good manners.' He was trying to sound stern, I could tell, but a hard cock was pressed against my belly, and he sounded more amused and aroused than upset. 'This will hurt you a lot more than it does me.' At that cheesy line, I knew that, while this spanking was a correction, and would sting, it was also meant to be a little fun.

My bare ass tingled in anticipation.

His big hand smacked down, no gentle warm-up here, but a hard blow at what must have been close to his full strength. I yelped and tried to jump away, but, with Darren's other arm holding me in place, I wasn't going anywhere.

Just as the sting started to segue into pleasure, he struck again. Ten times more his hand rained down, not giving me enough time to process the sensation. I kicked so hard one of my shoes went flying, and squirmed, and shrieked. I think my clit got involved too, but the sting was too strong, too shocking, to process well into pleasure. I could feel my sex and upper thighs were slick with moisture, but my brain was mostly focused on the hurt. At number ten, which reverberated through my bones, I yelled, 'Fuck, fuck, fuck!'

'Language,' Darren murmured and spanked me hard three more times – one, I suppose, for each 'fuck'.

He let me rest a bit, one hand stroking my hair, the other teasing at my hot, overly sensitive buns.

Then he drew me up so I was straddling his lap and wrapped his arms around me. 'Good girl,' he said. 'Good, brave girl. Thank you for taking the correction so well, even if you had to curse a bit. Now we'll get on to the fun stuff.'

He kissed me tenderly.

Two things happened that startled me and probably startled him too.

I burst into tears, sobbing as if I'd lost my best friend. No, as if I'd found my best friend after thinking we'd never see each other again.

And, through the tears, I came with a screamed 'yes' and a squirt that condemned Darren's elegant trousers to the dry cleaners.

I ruined his shirt, too; he didn't want to let me go

long enough to grab tissues, so I ended up wiping my eyes and blowing my nose on that fine cotton. 'I didn't know,' I whispered, unable to meet his eyes, 'how much I craved that. I mean I knew, but ...'

'The reality's always a surprise. I knew I fantasised about disciplining a woman I cared about, then comforting her, but I didn't know how right it would feel until I did it.' He kissed me again, first on my red nose, then on my lips. 'Welcome home to the fifties, Gina.'

'I think I'll like it here.'

He nudged me off his lap and on to my feet. 'Come on then.'

'What?' Clearly my brain wasn't working properly yet.

'We're going to the bedroom. That was just a little spanking to get you back in line. Now it's time for the fun, sensual spanking. And then I want to end the night deep inside you.'

How could I argue with that?

The Copy Typist's Tale
Lisette Ashton

'Seriously,' Donald concluded, holding up a warning finger to emphasise the importance of the moment, 'if it happens again, I'm going to spank you.'

There was no trace of a smile on his lips. There was no suggestion of humour in his demeanour. Maxine could tell he was totally, thoroughly and completely pissed off. But it seemed incongruous for him to be making flirtatious jokes about spanking while expressing his disapproval over the spelling mistakes she had made in his stupid article on stupid Chaucer.

'Spanking,' she repeated. The word felt heavy in her mouth. It sounded inappropriate in the academic formality of Donald's office. It sounded completely wrong and out of place.

'I'll spank you,' he promised. 'I'll have you bent over this desk. I'll have your knickers pulled down to your ankles. And I'll stripe your bare backside until it's red raw. Do you understand me?'

He pointed to a plaque behind the desk. There was a cane mounted on the plaque. It was an old schoolmaster's cane bent into a menacing arc. The cane sat beneath the engraved words 'Speak softly and carry a big stick'.

'I'll use my old cane to stripe your backside if you do this again,' he warned. 'Do you understand me?'

Maxine nodded. She didn't bother waiting for him to dismiss her from the room. Instead, she backed out of his office and disappeared to the sanctuary and security of her own workstation. Her cheeks were burning crimson. Her eyes stung with the threat of tears. And she despised the way his threat had been simultaneously hateful and exciting.

Of course, the problem was not of her own making. She blamed the stupid professor. She blamed stupid Chaucer. She blamed the stupid administration cuts.

She blamed the software that was supposed to conduct a spellcheck.

The software underlined incorrect and unfamiliar words with a squiggly red line. And, while this was probably a useful tool for most offices in the university, it happened to be a tremendous burden in this branch of the English Literature department.

Professor Donald White was a lecturer in Middle English. He was in the process of compiling an exhaustive and comprehensive series of lectures and course-notes to explain his thoughts on the original texts of Chaucer's *Canterbury Tales*. And for Maxine, who had fudged her way through Chaucer when she scraped her mediocre degree a decade earlier, the arcane language remained a bewildering mystery.

Ordinarily the conflict between the professor's specialist language and her own ignorance would not have presented a problem. But the university had made extensive administration cuts. Maxine's new duties included all that she had done previously as well as the secretarial requirements left by the voluntary redundancy of Professor White's former secretary Adele. And, as she brooded on his threat to administer a spanking, Maxine wondered if the responsibilities were proving too much.

She sniffed back a tear.

'What's the problem?'

Jacqueline May stood over her. Jacqueline, who had the cubicle next to Maxine's, had been with the university for the best part of a century and had spent every working day in the faculty of Middle English Literature.

'It's Professor White,' Maxine explained. She stopped herself from crying but it took a serious effort. 'He was really cross. I'd been typing up his articles on the stupid *Canterbury Tales* and I made a mistake.'

Jacqueline winced.

Maxine pretended not to notice. 'Professor White said he'll spank me if I make another mistake.' She glanced up at Jacqueline and studied the woman's old but kindly face. 'He sounded serious.'

Jacqueline pursed her lips. 'Call his bluff.'

'Call his –'

Jacqueline put a hand on hers. 'I'm giving you the same advice I gave to your predecessor a decade ago,' she explained. 'Adele hadn't been a week working for Professor White. She was sitting in this same room and complaining to me that White had given her a dressing down for spelling something wrong in one of his dull and dreary articles about five-hundred-year-old stories. She told me that he'd threatened to spank her. And I told her to call his bluff.'

Maxine considered this. 'Did it work?'

Jacqueline shrugged. 'Adele was ready to walk out of here that night when she spoke to me. After I'd told her to call his bluff, she spent another ten years working for him. Does that sound to you like it worked?'

It was a compelling argument. And, the more she thought about it, the more Maxine realised she wanted to call the professor's bluff and see how he would respond. She glanced at the paperwork in her in-tray and realised there was another of his articles waiting for her attention.

Ordinarily, the sight of so much complicated typing forced a knot of despair to tighten in her stomach. But this time, knowing she could exploit the situation to her advantage, she found herself smiling as she placed the sheets of handwritten paper into her copy holder.

'I'll have you bent over this desk. I'll have your knickers pulled down to your ankles. And I'll stripe your bare backside until it's red raw. Do you understand me?'

The memory of White's words echoed through her thoughts. It was almost as though he had re-whispered the threat in her ear. She despised the way the words made her sex lips moist. She didn't want to be aroused by the threat of the professor's physical punishment. But it was impossible to escape the lewd arousal the situation awoke in her.

He was a handsome man.

She suspected he was in his early fifties, although there was an ageless appeal to him. His hair was gunmetal grey, shot through with flecks of silver over the temples. The fact that he always wore a charcoal suit, and was never seen without a Windsor-knotted tie at his throat, added to the air of cool, efficient authority that he always exuded. And she guessed it was because she found him attractive and desirable that his threats of physical punishment were so stinging.

She typed the title of the article he had requested: *The Knight's Tale.*

94

And, while it was usual for her to censoriously self-check every word she wrote, Maxine realised she was rereading the title trying to discover if there was a word she could deliberately misspell.

Frustratingly, she couldn't see a way to make a deliberate typo in the title without the effort seeming too obvious. Frowning, she turned to the opening quotation. A smile broke her lips as she read:

WHILOM, AS OLDE STORIES TELLEN US,
THER WAS A DUC THAT HIGHTE THESEUS ...

She typed.

Well, as old stories tell us,
There was a duck that high Theses.

The lines made her stomach tighten. In the original version the computer underlined seven of the words with its familiar red squiggle. In her amended version there were no red squiggles. Admittedly, it made less sense now that she understood every word. It had made more sense when it was written in unintelligible Middle English. She was particularly puzzled by the reference in *The Knight's Tale* to a duck. But she didn't bother trying to dwell on those details. It was enough to know that Professor White would be furious.

And, if he intended following through with his threat, she knew this would be the translation that made him summon her to his office.

She worked for an hour on the article. Before leaving for the evening, Jacqueline checked in to see if she had recovered from her earlier upset. Maxine dismissed her with a curt nod and the assurance that she was following Jacqueline's advice. She was determined that everything in the article, with the exception of those opening two lines, would be a flawless reiteration of Professor White's thoughts on *The Knight's Tale*.

And, as soon as it was finished, she read swiftly through the work and then sent it to the printer. She snatched the warm pages from the still humming machine, tapped them neatly together and then marched them briskly to White's office.

He was still sitting behind his desk. He wore a pair of heavily framed reading glasses and the white gloves of a curator. With a frown of concentration, he pored over a huge and ancient dusty volume from the university's extensive library of original mediaeval texts. He didn't as much as glance up when she placed the pages in the centre of the volume.

Infuriated by his inattention, Maxine turned on her heel and flounced out of the door. She rushed back to her cubicle and glowered at the empty offices. He should have been outraged by the way she placed the typed pages in the centre of the open book he was reading. He should have been furious at her lack of consideration in bursting into his office and ignoring all the usual rigours of protocol.

'I'll have you bent over this desk. I'll have your knickers pulled down to your ankles. And I'll stripe your bare backside until it's red raw. Do you understand me?'

Instead of acting on that threat, he had acted as though she wasn't there.

She squeezed one hand into a fist. The pressure of her fingernails against the palm produced a bright twist of satisfaction. If she squeezed her hand a little more tightly, she knew she would draw blood. The idea was so tempting it was almost irresistible. But she stopped herself from falling back into that habit.

Instead, she reached for her coat and her car keys and prepared to make her way home. It was a depressing and unsatisfying conclusion to the evening. There remained an unsated longing in her loins which she knew had been caused by Professor White and his threat to administer retribution. But if he wasn't going to respond to the challenge she had laid down, she knew her position was going to remain maddeningly unsatisfied.

The intercom on her desk rang.

She snatched a sharp breath of surprise. The intercom rang for a second time and she contemplated ignoring it – to see how White would be able to show his anger at her if she refused to communicate with him. The idea did not last long. Warily, she picked up the telephone handset. 'Hello?'

'Maxine?'

She swallowed. 'Professor White.'

'Could you come into my office, please?'

She held her breath for a beat. 'Is there a problem, Professor White?'

'Could you come into my office, Maxine? I'd like to discuss the article you kindly typed for me.' He said nothing more. The line went dead.

She stiffened. Glancing around the office, noticing that hers was the only occupied cubicle on this late November evening, Maxine wondered if she had made a mistake. White had threatened her with physical punishment. Instead of reporting it, she had provoked him with another document with deliberate mistakes. And now she was alone in the building with him.

Her bowels tightened as she stood up.

She walked slowly to his office. In her hands she held a notepad and pen, as though the pages could offer some defence against the professor's wrath. This time, when she arrived at his door, she knocked and waited to be summoned before she entered the room.

'Come in.'

The air was thick and electric with anticipation. Maxine's stomach folded when she saw the professor.

98

He stood in front of his desk. And, in his hands, he held the cane that had been mounted on his wall.

He flexed the cane into an arc.

'Professor White?' she began hesitantly.

'Do you recall what I said would happen if you made another mistake?'

'You said you would …' She paused, then swallowed. 'You said you would *spank* me.' The word came out sounding strangled.

'Did you think it was an idle threat?'

'I– I –'

He spoke over the stammering response she had been about to make. 'Stand at my desk, Maxine.'

She went to the desk. The ancient volume had been removed. All that remained on the desk were the pages she had sent from the printer. The opening lines glared accusingly up at her from the top of the first page. She blinked back tears of self-recrimination. Her cheeks blazed bright pink with embarrassment.

'Read out the lines from the top of the page you've written.'

She drew a deep breath and then began determinedly. '*Well, as old stories tell us, there was a duck that high Theses.*'

He slashed his cane through the air. It made a sound like the snapping of an autumn twig. Maxine bit back a cry of surprise.

'Bend over,' White snapped. 'Lift up your skirt. Pull down your panties. Prepare to be properly punished for this – just as I warned you.'

She opened her mouth to protest but words refused to come out. She was alone in a room with a professor threatening to stripe her backside and, instead of finding a voice to tell him that he couldn't treat her this way, she was only able to work her mouth soundlessly – and wonder what the lash of the cane would feel like against her bare backside. She refused to accept that a part of her wanted to find out whether the pain would be as exciting as she expected.

'This is how it should have read,' Professor White began. He didn't bother picking up a text. Clearly the prologue from *The Knight's Tale* was sufficiently well known for him to recite it from memory. Turning his back to her, he said softly, '*Whilom, as olde stories tellen us, ther was a duc that highte Theseus ...*'

Without turning back to face her, he said, 'I'm going to stripe your bare backside once for each mistake you made in those opening lines.'

She swallowed the coppery taste of her own fear.

'If, when I turn round, you aren't in the position that I told you – bent over my desk, skirt raised, knickers down – then I'll have you dismissed from the university and you'll never work here again. If you are in the position I instructed, then we can begin your punishment. Do you understand?'

She muttered a breathless agreement.

And, at the same time, she tugged her knickers down to her ankles and hoisted her skirt up as she bent over his desk. The shame struck her with a fury that churned her stomach. Her cheeks burned a bright crimson that she knew would simmer tears if they started to fall down her face. She was bent over the professor's desk, thrusting her bare backside into the air, with her ankles straining against the elasticated waistband of her fallen knickers. She wouldn't let herself think about the image that she was presenting to him because it was too raw and sexual a posture of submission for her to contemplate without sweltering beneath her own arousal.

'Good.'

He had turned to face her. He was admiring her bare bottom. Inwardly, Maxine groaned.

'I see you've followed my instructions this time.' With haughty disdain he added, 'It shows that you can be useful for some things.'

He was walking towards her. The cane rested lazily in his hand. He used it to point at the pages on the desk and tapped the top two lines. 'Read what you've written here. Read it one word at a time. I shall stripe you for each mistake you've made.'

'But –'

'That's not how it begins,' he snapped. He slashed the cane across the flat expanse of her buttocks.

Maxine held her breath. At first there was no sensation at all. She heard the whip-like crack of the cane. She felt the pressure of the supple wood pressing against her rear.

But there was no immediate pain.

It was only in the moments afterwards that the shock of stinging pain rushed through her. A blazing line of heat seared her buttocks. The sensation was almost like the spark of an electric bite spiking at flesh. She held her breath, petrified he would hear her squeal in response.

'Begin again, please,' White said coolly.

She took a steadying breath. Blinking tears from her eyes she read, 'Well.'

He slashed the cane across her cheeks. This time she felt the pain as soon as the wood kissed her backside. It was a bright and sharp sting that made her eyes grow wide. Hatefully, as well as supplying the most humiliating pain she had ever suffered, it also made the centre of her sex growl with a warm and longing need.

'The next word,' White prompted.

'As.' She spat the word for him and hated the way it sounded like a sob.

White nodded his approval. He urged her to continue, pointing to the next word with the tip of his cane.

'Old.'

He stepped behind her. 'Is that *old* with an "e" on the end?'

She bit her lower lip. 'No,' she whispered.

The cane hissed as it sliced through the air. When it landed against her rear, she could almost hear the sizzle of flesh as it crackled beneath the heat of the cane's punishing force. The impact left her breathless and close to tears. It also made her hatefully aware of the dull heat that now warmed the inner muscles of her sex.

'Continue,' White insisted.

Maxine blinked the tears from her eyes and read the next word from the page. 'Stories,' she managed.

From the corner of her eye she could see White nodding approval.

Bravely, she went on. 'Tell –'

There was a moment's hesitation. It was a moment when she thought he had decided that the punishment had gone too far. Or, she thought afterwards, it was a moment when he was possibly waiting for another syllable from her. And then the cane was sparking another line of red agony across her backside. She whimpered softly, biting back the shriek she wanted to bellow into the otherwise silent office. The cheeks of her backside felt raw and ravaged and cruelly tortured. The centre of her sex was now a throbbing pulse of greedy need.

'Not *tell*,' White said mildly. 'The word is *tellen*. It derives from the Old English word *tellan*. It's a verb that means either *to count* or, in this instance, *to tell*.'

She blinked as though registering these facts. In truth,

his words had simply allowed her a moment to catch her breath and fight back the threat of delighted tears she wanted to release.

White tapped the page again. The tip of his cane pressed on the next word.

'Us.'

She held her breath. She had forgotten which of the words she was reading were correct and which were spelling mistakes. When White gave her a smiling nod of approval, she almost melted for him. He really was attractive. And, while the punishment was harsh and extreme, it wasn't the worst way to spend an evening at work.

'There,' she read for him.

'Is that *there* with an "e" on the end?'

'Yes.'

The cane bit sharply across her rear. This time she hissed in shock. She suspected that White had been laying the lines across her backside with deliberate precision. In her mind's eye she could picture lines as meticulous stripes: each one bright red and straight against the pale curve of her buttock. This was the first time it felt as though the cane was landing on previously punished flesh. She imagined her backside now looked like a five-barred gate with one diagonal slashing crossing over the previous four lines. The severity of the pain was so powerful she squeezed her eyes against the threat of tears.

And, to her dismay, she could feel the trickle of syrupy

wetness begin to spill from the juicy centre of her sex. The arousal seemed like it was complete. She was bent over, suffering the maddening heat of White's punishment, and wallowing in the sultry warmth of her own arousal. She knew it would only take a single finger to caress the tip of her clitoris and her climax would be swift and brutal and unrelenting.

White tapped his cane against the page.

She drew a faltering breath before reading the word for him. She could taste the flavour of her sex filling the air as she inhaled. The scent was pungent and powerful and a strong reminder of how exciting she had found this experience.

'Was.'

He nodded curtly.

'A.'

He smiled for her to continue.

'Duck –'

The blow was so sharp and sudden it took her breath away. The sting seared like a white-hot razor. The pain was a blazing, burning, brutal fuse to her arousal. Even as she was biting back the groan of despair she could feel the wave of sexual release welling through her loins and threatening to burst from her sopping sex lips.

'It should have been D-U-C.'

Maxine could hear the tone of barely restrained anger in his voice.

'Chaucer would have pronounced it *Duke*,' White went on. 'And you've written it as though I'm appraising the *Canterbury Tales* according to Donald-fucking-Duck.' He slashed the cane against her rear three more times.

She rushed through the final three words.

There was nothing wrong with the word *that*. But the penultimate word should have been *highte*. White told her it was a Middle English word that translated roughly as *was called*. She wasn't really listening. She was focusing solely on escaping from the room before she suffered the embarrassment of climaxing on his desk.

'The final word should have been *Theseus* not *theses*.'

Maxine couldn't even hear the difference.

White delivered a succession of sharp stinging blows for each of those mistakes. The impact left her bewildered. But it also left her determined about what her course of action should be.

Her sex was dripping with arousal.

The need for satisfaction nestled in her loins like an unspoken need. She was sure, if she simply pressed a hand against her labia, the orgasm would be certain, instantaneous and enormously satisfying. It was a theory she wanted to test as soon as she was out of White's office. She could picture herself locked in a cubicle of the university's staff toilets, pressing cool fingers against her warm flesh, and groaning through the release of multiple orgasms.

The idea made her muscles clench eagerly.

'You have every right to go and report me to the Dean,' Professor White said calmly. 'The way I've just spanked your backside is nothing more than unnecessary physical cruelty and I'm sure I violated your human rights as well as quite a few legal rights including actual bodily harm and sexual assault. If you feel the need to report me, I'd suggest you go and do it now while every detail is still fresh in your mind and all the evidence is still fresh on your ...' He paused. His fingers traced over the searing heat of the stripes on her backside.

Maxine stiffened and realised that a minor thrill of release had melted through her body as she endured the touch of his hand on her flesh. It was the most exquisite sensation she could ever recall experiencing.

White cleared his throat. 'If you feel the need to report me,' he repeated, 'I'd suggest you do it now while every detail is still fresh.'

'Thank you for informing me of my rights,' she said dully.

Her skirt fell naturally into place as soon as she stood up. She picked up her notepad and pen. Her knickers were still around her ankles but she refused to suffer the indignity of bending down to pick them up. It was easier to simply step out of them and leave them on his carpet.

'Will there be anything else, Professor White?' she asked.

'No.' He said the word stiffly. 'That will be all for this evening. There is another article waiting in my out-tray but it's late now so I'm sure that will wait until tomorrow morning.'

Maxine snatched the pages from his out-tray and headed back to her desk. She wanted to go to the privacy of the ladies' toilets so she could release the unsated need that lingered in her loins. But, instead, she wanted to show White that she was a match for his demanding response to her spelling mistakes.

She sat heavily in front of the computer, savouring the sensation of her searing backside pressing against the seat. Glancing at the front page of White's second article, she realised he was continuing with his dissection of Chaucer. Deliberately, she typed the title of the piece into a new document:

THE MILLINER'S TALE.

The Holiday
Poppy St Vincent

North London, June, Dusk

Finally the door clicked behind him. Anna had never known one man take so long to get himself out to the gym as her husband. He made more false starts than a primary school egg-and-spoon race. Still, he was gone now and his study was unguarded.

Anna stood outside his door and shook a little. There was precious little reason for her shaking. David was not the sort of man to make his wife shake. He was an editor but she was not one of his authors. She was his wife. It was perfectly normal for her to go and tidy his office. She opened the door.

Anna moved quietly, as though he were still in the house, and every time she heard a sound she stopped mouse-still. As she started to open his computer and wait for it to let her in, she supposed that she could just ask him to let her look at his work and say, 'David, you don't know this, but you know those spanking books you edit? Well, I would love to be spanked. You know the sort of thing? Call me naughty and tip me over your knee; and would you like me to dress as a schoolgirl or a maid? So, if you wouldn't mind, I will just read them and then you could pretend to catch me and punish me for it.'

Anna gave a tight little smile as she imagined the ridiculous scene. She could see with total clarity the inevitable look of disgust on his handsome face. She could never bear his disapproval. She hung her head for a moment, her pretty blonde bob falling forward as the pout of resignation came to her lips.

It was not hard to find the stories. There they were, rows upon rows of them, all tucked-up like toy soldiers in his documents file. There, she found the author she always hunted out when David left her alone with his work, Michael Marsters.

As a child and an avid reader, Anna would often get lost in a book for hours. At such times, she would lose the rest of the world and exist solely in the pages in front of her, which is exactly how David found her.

It took her several minutes to realise he was there. The story in front of her, with a rugged cowboy and a tempestuous heroine who got put in her place by his large rough hands, had prevented her from hearing the front door, his call of hello or his steps on the stairs.

It was his shoes she noticed first. The end of a chapter fell near the bottom of the screen and she paused in her reverie to detect a pair of familiar dark leather brogues that made her feel ill. Her mind, the coward, had gone elsewhere and left her to face David alone.

'I was just catching up on your new book, about trees ... I mean the one you are writing yourself for a change. You don't mind, I know. I love the way you write about the woods; the forests. Very evocative.' She looked up and smiled. 'Anyway, good workout? Shall I get dinner started?' She kept talking as he walked behind her so they could gaze at the screen together. 'I was thinking steaks, I could make a sauce.' Her voice got softer as the sentence fell into disuse. All she could see on the screen were words like 'spank', 'red' and 'swollen'.

Anna looked at David's desk as she tucked her arms in front of her. 'Would you like some dinner now?' she said very quietly to his keyboard.

David put one hand on either side of her, flat on the desk, and put his cold cheek next to her flushed one. He was so tall that he felt like a cave bear towering over her.

'Anna? Is there anything you would like to say to me?' His voice was as quiet as hers but he had a very different tone.

She shook her head softly and tried to draw herself in at the shoulders. She thought maybe, if he could not feel her, he would forget she was there, the quiet child at bedtime. Slowly she watched the desk leave her to be replaced by David's face as he gently swung the chair around towards him.

With one finger he brought her crimson face up to meet his grey eyes. 'Anna?'

And that is how Anna got her first spanking. It was slow, calm and interspersed with a conversation about respect, trust and privacy. It was not how she imagined it. Her husband's hands were smooth and soft but the sound and sting they made took her breath away. She held her hands over her face the whole time as she dangled forward over his knee and did not even have the courage to ask him to stop.

* * *

Somewhere in the woods of Ontario, August, Early Evening

'Christ, would you just light the bloody barbeque.'

It sounded like a prayer and it had the whispered tone of one, but that was more to save her skin than her soul. Charlotte slammed the knife down, giving the spring onions a brief reprieve as she went into her husband's study. She internalised her frustration as she eyed him bent over his laptop, engrossed in his writing. With a studied tone of patience, she said, 'Honey, would you mind starting the barbeque? They'll be here in an hour and it needs to warm up before I put the potatoes on.'

She heard the keys stop tapping moments before he looked up. Their eyes met, and a flicker of understanding passed between them. His dark eyes held her green ones and one brown eyebrow rose.

'Stay right there,' he instructed, his large form moving past her and from the room before she had a chance to reply.

She really did not have time for this. She looked at the clock and sighed. He was so frustrating; he had no idea what it was like to feed people or to have guests. He liked the evening that she created. He liked the food which she had planned, bought, prepared and served. He just had to smile and pour wine. Charlotte knew she had done nothing wrong and her husband was just being a selfish idiot. She would tell him so (in a more subtle manner) and he would apologise. She heard him return and she realised, with no small surprise, that she had done as he had instructed. She did not even turn to face the door as he came back into the room.

'Did you put it on, Mike?'

'I did.'

He stood behind her, breathing in the smell of her hair

as he stood close enough to rub her bottom gently under her shorts. He loved having a summer home in all this Canadian heat. His wife smelled of summer and she was always about four items of clothing away from naked. He smiled as he saw the certainty and tension in her shoulders. Her head was high, facing the window in front of her as if she were looking at the woods that stretched out twenty feet from their cabin. But Mike knew better.

He knew his wife was steaming mad. She was so full of nerves and pressure to perform that she had been using her clipped bossy work voice with him all afternoon. But now was the time to help her calm down.

Mike stepped one pace to his left and, placing his right hand against the front of her tight tanned thighs, moved her a step backwards. At the same time he slowly bent her trim figure down at a right angle until her elbows rested on his desk. He made a lax attempt to hold back his gentle laugh at her small explosion of impatience and rage.

'For God's sake, Mike, you can be such an idiot sometimes.' She tried to stand up so they could have more of an equal conversation but he had kept his heavy hand on her back and she was stuck talking to his stupid blue deck-shoes.

She sighed and used her very best reasonable tone. 'Mike, I know you think an evening like this just does itself –' She paused as she felt his right hand travel up her body and start to unbutton her shorts. 'But it just doesn't. He is your editor, you have no idea how stressful this is, you have no idea …' Her voice went up in a little shriek as she felt him tug down her shorts taking her knickers with them. It remained high as she continued, 'I just want it to be nice for everyone. I have spent days on this– OW! You are such a jerk!

By this point he had placed four smart slaps on her pale cheeks. And she was trying hard to stand up. 'You need to listen, you are being unfair. You have to stop! OW! Now!'

He had not paused but continued to slap her bottom as she talked, the sound hitting against the plain walls of his room and going through the screen door to the woodland creatures outside.

'I am listening,' he explained as he inspected his handi-work. 'Keep talking.'

The solemn spanks continued, setting a steady pace that she tried to ignore as she went on, 'Do you know what? You can cook in future. You can do all the bloody work and I will just sit here and complain if you get uptight … please just bloody stop doing that.' She stamped her foot twice, to punctuate her demands.

Instead of complying, he upped the tempo and the force of his strikes, covering her bottom from the top of its curve and down to her thighs. He watched her try to twist her naked hot bum away from him, a futile but amusing habit of hers, causing him to lean down over her and whisper in her ear, 'Straighten your back and stay still unless you want me to take my belt off.'

Charlotte cast a fearful look to her left – trust him to still be wearing jeans with a ruddy leather belt in this heat. Waves crashed over her, early signs of inevitable defeat as she shuffled back as she had been told. Then she felt an unwanted longing for him to show her that strip of brown leather sliding through the loops of his jeans, and a deep, wordless settling down as she waited for him to take her where he would.

She continued to cry out as his large hard hand struck her over and over. She forgot about the meal, the timings, her guests and anything other than her husband's unrelenting punishment. The sound, the sharp pain, the terrible heat in her bum, all became elements of her contrition.

He stopped when he stopped. She had no idea what it was that told him it was enough, but by then she would have taken whatever he had given her.

He took her into him and, resting his chin on her blonde hair, he kissed her.

'I want a cuddle,' she told his T-shirt and found herself transferred to his lap as he sat on the sofa at the side of his study. She shuffled around awkwardly, trying to keep her swollen bum off his thighs, pointing it towards the open window and smiling as he covered it with his hand to hold her close to him. 'I'm sorry, I'm just scared. I just want it to be great and also, also, what if ...'

'What, honey?'

'What if they are like us? Or, worse, what if they're not?'

She could feel his quizzical expression even though he made no sound.

'Well, you write rude stories about this sort of stuff,' she said, wriggling her bum against his hand, 'and he is your editor.' She lowered her voice to a whisper. 'He probably guesses you sometimes spank me and other more awful things. I am pretty certain he knows.'

She looked up at Mike in time to see him shrug. His usually short dark hair was starting to get long and fell forward over his right eyebrow. She pushed it back off his face, insisting, 'Mike, Mike, it matters. What if he knows?'

To interrupt her, Mike tilted her back so that she rested in his right arm, holding her off the floor with his strength alone and forcing her to hold on to his neck to keep herself steady.

'Let me up –' she began, but she was interrupted again with a kiss, a full passionate intense kiss that made her forget what she had been about to object to. She let go of his neck and let her hands rest on his T-shirt as she returned his kiss, her lips parted and her breath quickened.

Mike pulled back a little and looked down at his wife. 'I know,' he said, 'and you know. That's what matters, nothing else.'

She pulled herself up to his mouth again. 'But, Mike, can't we ... can't you ... can't I?' A thousand erotic offerings poured from her eyes. 'Please.'

He smiled and shook his head. She would be concentrating all night on how much she wanted him. Her distraction would be perfect for her. Later, much later, she would wrap her lips, her whole self around him. He could be patient too.

Mike stood up, placing his petulant wife on her feet. He noted her huffing and puffing as she trekked back to the kitchen, and made sure he had a glower ready for when she turned around to check if he heard.

After forty minutes of chopping, arranging, dish-selecting, candle-lighting and other military-style preparations, Charlotte gave herself fifteen minutes for a lightning shower and makeup. It was so exciting to have guests from home, to hear the familiar accents, but at the same time it made her nervous. She had made their bedroom up as far away from the master bedroom as she could, but it was only for two days and even she could evade a spanking for that time.

She eyed herself sternly as she applied nude eye shadow and barely there foundation. It was easier to get made up now she had a tan, she thought. These people are in

118

a foreign country and will be just delightful, she assured herself. David and Anna will be polite and sweet and English like us. Propriety will not allow anything un-vanilla to sneak in. It will be a lovely evening.

However, the idea of the husband being like Mike was one she could not shift. What if Mike said something to her in front of their guests? What if he threatened to spank her and the others stayed and watched? What if Anna was cheeky? Mike often put Charlotte in the corner before and after a spanking. What would it be like to see that happen to another girl? What if Charlotte said something cheeky to David? Would he tell her off?

But no, these were disturbing thoughts. These things will not happen. Charlotte tried to quell her nerves as she sprayed her favourite perfume to remind her of happy memories. It will be a lovely evening.

The peaceful effect of her mantra was somewhat spoiled by the sound of car tyres on the drive and Charlotte snapped her lipstick into its case with a quiet 'Fuckity fuck'. She smiled what she hoped was a confident smile at the mirror and made sure to shut the door on the clothing carnage of their bedroom as she left.

David was just as Mike had described him, so tall he had to stoop as he entered their house, but he was graceful in his movements and gracious in his manners. He had an easy laugh and arrived full of compliments for their house. 'Just wonderful,' he exclaimed in the neat vowel sounds of home. 'Perfect seclusion, woods behind you and lake to the front of you. You have it all. What we wouldn't do for this kind of privacy, eh, Anna?'

Charlotte smiled weakly as Mike hustled them in and poured gin and tonics for everyone. Lots of people want privacy and David wrote too, she was sure. Privacy is a writing thing, nothing more sinister.

His wife, Anna, was just like a Victorian beauty from one of the pictures Mike so adored. She was a honey blonde, a deeper shade than Charlotte's sun-lightened hair, and her lips were naturally dark pink and bee-stung. She had a gentle chuckle which came easily to her and she had arrived laden with English delicacies (Marmite and Yorkshire tea) that Canada for all its majesty could not provide. She was also keen, despite Charlotte's protests, to help in the kitchen.

Anna did her best to be helpful. Pooh-poohing any suggestion of jet-lag, she dressed and tossed the salad and cut more limes for gin and tonics as Charlotte tidied the kitchen. There was a pause as both women realised they should join the men. Then for reasons neither explained they started a new conversation about airports, airlines and the coffee shops of Toronto while staying firmly in the kitchen.

Their peace was disturbed by Mike's casual entrance. Considerably shorter than David, he had a muscular frame and Anna's attention was drawn to his tanned, thick forearms as he wrapped one arm around his wife sitting at the counter.

'Charlotte? Would you and Anna like to join us, do you think?' Mike winked at his wife and did not appear to notice Anna's wide-eyed alarm at his arrival.

The meal was easy and relaxed; drink and conversation flowed. Tales of Canadian life, of moose, bears and the idiosyncrasies of living in a new country were exchanged with the petty politics of London living. There was scarcely a moment of silence in the whole meal as Anna and Charlotte, giddy with words, introduced topics and conversational gambits with the skill of professional hostesses. It was not until the end of the main course when they left together to clear the plates and bring dessert that the men had a chance to talk.

Laden as they were and laughing off the men's offers of help, they carried trays to the kitchen and carefully placed them on the counter. Anna unloaded the trays as Charlotte loaded the dishwasher.

'Where did I leave my bag?' Anna scrabbled around under where her coat had been hung up. 'Oh, thank God,' she sighed, as she unwrapped a little tablet of gum and placed it on her tongue.

'Nicorette,' she explained to a bemused Charlotte. 'I'm just dying for a smoke but you know how uptight these men can get. I mean, if yours is anything like mine ...' Her sentence spluttered and died.

They both knew just what she meant. Their eyes caught and wrestled themselves free in a moment.

'Just don't get caught, that's my rule,' Charlotte replied with a weak smile.

This is how it would start. This was Anna's plan. It was just like one of Mike's stories, the schoolgirl having a smoke and being caught. Charlotte took a deep breath and mentally regrouped.

'Let's take pudding out. You go ahead and I will follow with coffee.'

To her relief, Anna agreed and that storyline, as far as Charlotte could see, had been curtailed.

They sat in the gazebo surrounded on three sides by deep woods. 'You must love it here,' Anna said, as she leaned back in her chair full of lemon-and-lime tart.

Charlotte looked longingly at Anna's manicured nails as she listened to Mike describe the sounds of wolves. 'And of course,' Mike went on, 'the forests are filled with inspiration.'

Charlotte dropped her spoon with a clatter. She knew from bitter experience that the woods were filled with switches. She blushed and looked at her skirt. They were surrounded by switches; the thought would not let her go. She caught Anna looking at her.

To Charlotte's horror, David said, 'I couldn't agree more, there is so much potential in woods like these. They must go on for hundreds of miles. It is the total isolation, the way people could do anything in there and no one would ever know. It isn't the privacy; it's a dangerous kind of freedom, something atavistic. It can make you see time in a totally new way, as though there is no past or future; time can't exist where there is no human influence to witness it.'

Oh, for God's sake, thought Charlotte, he is just like Mike. And I bet she is too. She saw Anna looking adoringly at her husband; one of those 'let's pretend we live years ago when every wife got spanked and the world was all better' looks.

'Mike, Anna is a big fan of your work,' David said, clearly not wanting to talk about his book. Besides, he wanted to let Anna see that the world would not fall in if they talked about the specialist books that drew them together.

Charlotte gave an imperceptible nod to herself, her fears confirmed. They were all in on it. They were here to surprise her. Mike was adopting a look of surprise all too quickly and even Anna was blushing in embarrassment at the obvious plan.

Anna, meanwhile, who had been finally feeling safe as her husband had been describing his new work, the totally vanilla book about trees, was caught between the devil and the deep blue sea. If she denied her admiration for Mike's work, she appeared rude to their hosts; admit it and she'd die of shame. As she watched a hummingbird disappear into the trees, she wished she could vanish with it. Desperate for something to say, she blurted, 'It is just such a beautiful spot, isn't it, Charlotte? Do you feed the hummingbirds to attract them?'

Just as eager to change the subject, Charlotte said, 'It is, and we do. We have a pot of honey water, well, not quite a pot. It is a thingy. A thingy of water. Would you like to see it?'

Anna hardly noticed the clipped response, but Mike heard it and his brow furrowed at his wife.

'I very much would,' Anna said hastily.

It was not that the women fluttered off like the birds that made the men smile, it was the totally unconscious way both women covered their bottoms with their hands as they did so.

Anna was spitting tacks. It was one massive set-up. They had all planned it. David had clearly told these two all about her and here they were on some bloody cliché of a holiday in the woods and she was supposed to just go along with it. Charlotte was clearly comfortable with the whole thing but Anna was not about to go there with her.

The women reached the far side of the cabin where they glared at each other, while the hummingbird feeding was left unappreciated.

Anna shook her head at Charlotte and turned away a little, giving a heavy sigh as she did so.

'What?' asked Charlotte.

Anna would not even look at her. Charlotte crossed her arms and glared. Anna saw it for herself: Charlotte was like Mike, she was going to try to be some sort of Topette. Her temper started to crack.

'Who the hell do you think you are? I don't know how long you have been out here, but if you think that we have come all the way to Canada ...'

She did not get any further as Charlotte kicked a watering can by her side. 'To waste your time?' Charlotte was being louder than she realised. 'To not even ask me or give me a choice. I am not here to be ... like that with just anyone.'

With so much to lose, neither woman would listen to the other. Neither could use the words they needed to, it was too much. There was simply no backing down from a confrontation they would not have. The idea of public humiliation was too much, the idea of being manipulated, of being forced down some bloody awful path where they would be a spectacle was too much. And the shouting escalated, bringing David and Mike to them just as it seemed the two women might have laid hands on one another.

The silence was as though pause had been pressed. Each woman was certain this was the moment that had been engineered by the other three. This was supremely unfair and would not be taken lying down.

Charlotte was about to start talking, before realising that was the action that would start events. No way would she be the trigger. She pointed her chin at Anna in a challenge.

Anna turned and glared at David. There was nothing she was prepared to say in front of Mike. She could see Mike's hands and his stupid big forearms. He even had a belt on like the man he wrote about in his story *Taming the Hellion* and she was not a hellion. She did yoga; hellions do not do yoga. So she stood next to David and held his hand waiting for the attention to move away from her.

Mike looked at Charlotte and then at David. 'I need to speak to Charlotte,' he told David. 'Would you excuse us?'

'Absolutely,' replied David who had not taken his eyes off Anna, his expression somewhere between rage and consternation.

In their room he let rip. 'What the hell is going on? I have no idea what is happening in your head tonight. What do you think you were doing?'

Anna, still shaken by her outburst, sat on the bed and bit her lip as he vented. In truth, she did not quite understand what had happened. She understood David even less; this was so unlike him. She did not answer any of his questions. She did not see what she could say that would not propel her into a worse spot.

As it was, saying nothing got her there just the same. Less than a minute later she was in the corner of the bedroom with her pretty lemon knickers at mid-thigh and her dress scrunched in her own hands in the small of her back. His firm instruction not to move suited her perfectly.

David said nothing as he sat on the bed to watch her. They talked a lot; they were talkers, it was what they did. Sometimes it was just a relief to hear the silence, to control the sound in the room.

Anna's shoulders hunched a little as she tried to hide herself in the corner; she could feel him looking at her. She wanted him not to. She wanted to be like the child who covers her eyes and the whole world disappears.

David liked this space. There was a kind of understanding in the silence that neither of them found with words. David protected the silence and the gifts it brought with his presence. Whatever came next would determine some part of their future; although Anna could not see it now, it was a test.

'Come here.' He spoke softly but the sudden noise made her start, a small flicker of surprise that betrayed her sense of fear about what was to come.

Anna kept her eyes down as she walked towards him, her hands still tugging at the dress she held behind her back; she only let go as David sat up to receive her over his lap. He lifted one leg to pin both of hers in place, angling her bottom up to provide a curved target. Her eyes shut tightly and Anna laid her head against the bed cover, noting the stitchwork of the quilt, a piece of Canada against her cheek.

'I am going to get your attention first,' he said as he rubbed her pale bottom, 'and then I think you will listen to me.'

She bit her lips against the obvious retort as the first hard slaps landed home. Each one was hot and she imagined each slap leaving a handprint as she tried to shift from side to side to get him to avoid the sorest areas. She was held so firmly by his leg that this movement was limited, a minuscule wriggle that pushed her more deeply against him. Each biting pain came announced, as by a toastmaster at a ball. 'They will hear us … David, stop, they will hear us.' This shame was as bad as the spanking and Anna started to claw away in earnest, using the end of the bed to try to get leverage away from the noise.

It took very little effort to keep her in place and his spanks increased in speed and strength. By then, she barely cared that they might be heard and begged him to stop. She reached back to hold his shirt in one hand as she really, honestly thought she could take no more.

The silence, when it came, took moments to reach her ears.

'Anna, you are going to stop fighting me about all of

128

this. You get so uptight about it, so tense about everything to do with spanking.' He saw her curl more tightly around him, a hot pink C around his waist. 'It makes it hard for you to function when you have this repressed urge within you. I know you say you don't want me to spank you, I know you say you don't want to live like the girls in the story.'

She made a small protest into the quilt. Her hand pushed a little, as though to move him away, but she did not let go. From somewhere else in the house, they heard a sharp crack and a woman's cry. Anna held on to David with more eagerness and waited for him to continue. Hearing Charlotte, although scary, told her what she needed to know.

'You don't have to ask me for this. I am taking all this choice away from you now. I knew how you felt and I thought it might help you to ask. But you can't or you won't and I am not waiting anymore. This is how we are now. This –' he gave her a hard, sudden spank that made her shriek '– is us now.'

He watched her closely and saw her back ease down into the bed, feeling the strength of her grip upon him. Her eyes had shot open when he started to speak and Anna smiled into the cover, a smile so deep, wide and true she did not know it was there at all.

On the other side of the house, Charlotte, bent over and waiting, had heard Anna's spanking. She squeezed one set of toes into a ball and then the other. This was not going to happen. This house was all about their privacy, it was all about letting them live however they wanted without worrying about being heard and here they were ... she could not think the rest of the sentence.

She laid her hand flat on the cool wood. Was this mahogany? She tried to remember; the colour was the same as if a rose had been made of wood. Behind her, her bottom was still there, naked, like a beacon. She tried to shift a little and received a hard (and terrifyingly loud) slap from the man sitting at his desk just a little to her left.

Her mouth opened to tell him to stop and then closed again without a word escaping. She did not want this to be worse. She tried to relax again; this was to be part of it, she knew. This waiting, in position, bared and just waiting for him to decide to act was the hardest bit. The sound of spanking stopped. Poor Anna, she would be so sore, her bum would be swollen and red. Charlotte imagined just how it would be.

It had been a hand spanking she had heard, so she imagined Anna over David's knee, dangling across it like a doll. His hand clamped around her waist, his large hand covering her bottom with each and every spank.

Charlotte tried to stand up. This is so wrong, this can't happen. None of this is acceptable. But she hardly moved. Three times she breathed in and out noisily before telling Mike how she felt.

'Mike.' She tried for more. She wanted to tell him that it was all wrong, that none of this is right at all. But all her words were confused and she could not work out what she meant anyway. She felt his hand rest on her bum, the heel of it pushing down a little where her cheeks curved and parted.

Charlotte knew herself well enough to know this desire. It was not her choice, it was who she was. She was bent over his desk at his order, waiting bare-bottomed for when he decided to punish her. She was listening for the sound of another girl being spanked. She had no intellectual response left; all she could do was part her legs a little and try to ignore the sensation that was growing in between them. She knew she had thought something very strongly, but she had forgotten it now. This waiting, this hand had taken her thoughts. She wanted him to ... she lost it again. She waited, sighing with frustration as his hand left her again and returned to his keyboard.

Mike stood and fetched the strap of leather that hung under his coat in the corner of his office. It was a gift from Charlotte years ago, bought on a trip to London. It had nearly killed her to buy it, and the embarrassment had been half the joy for him as he watched her shaking hands as she passed him the bag.

He smiled as he stood above her. His wife's curved back rose and fell as she breathed. Her bottom had tiny

131

goosebumps on it despite the warm evening. He could still make her mind him; he could still give her the feeling she had whispered to him years ago when they met. 'I want –' her breath hot in his ear as he held her tight in the dark '– I want you to make me feel like I am fourteen, like I have been caught, like I can't do anything about it.'

'Charlotte –' he brought them together with her name '– tell me why I am going to do this.' He laid the long black leather strap on the desk in front of her and wished he could see her eyes as she saw the threat.

'Mike, you don't have to do that. You don't have to do anything.'

'Sixteen,' he said.

'But I don't want you to. I was just stressed.'

'Thirty-two,' he said.

'But what about Anna? I think she was the problem and, if she had not been here, nothing would have happened at all.'

'Sixty-four.'

'Because I kicked off.' Her words pushed at each other as they rushed at him. 'Because I overreacted all night to Anna, to you, to David, and because I was rude to our guests and because –' the sadness inside her pushed a lone tear on to his desk to rest on the polished wood '– and because ... and because I am so confused about all this that it makes me behave like ... and I don't even know what I am confused about.'

As if to mark the pause, there was a flurry of spanks and pitiful squeals from Anna and David's room. Charlotte hid her head forward again and put her hands over her ears. She felt Mike stroking her back and she knew that it would not be long now.

'Charlotte, I want you to count each stroke and thank me. I know –' he spoke over her protest '– that you hate doing it. But, right now, I don't care what you like. You are going to accept every stroke, you are going to speak to me with respect and after this is over you are going to settle down and enjoy this weekend.

'Now, arch your back and present your bottom properly, young lady.'

Charlotte could feel her heart push against the wooden desk as she adopted the familiar position. She felt a little sick and was surprised at the relief she felt at being afraid of Mike. She started to wonder if it would be like this for ever when ...

'Ow! One, thank you, sir.' The strap landed across her bottom with a neat and accurate lick. It was one line she knew, and a moment later it was repeated. 'Argh! Thank you, sir.'

The pattern continued. Sometimes he would adopt a steady beat and she would be prepared but then he would change and she could not predict when the next line would come. Over and over he built burning strips across her pained cheeks and thighs until the two people fell into some kind of step. Charlotte found her place in the role of acceptance; even as it hurt and she wanted him to stop, she found herself existing in those stripes. She found herself meaning it as she thanked him.

Afterwards, so swollen and sore she did not want to move, so in his thrall she could not move, she stayed bent over the desk as he took her, slowly and with exquisite care as she bent in front of him, over the desk where he wrote.

Anna listened from the other room. In silence, Anna stood there, sore red bottom nowhere near as bright as her flushed cheeks as she listened to the sound of Charlotte being punished. At times, she made a little sound of distress, a sound which made David struggle against himself to call her to him, to bring her to bed and his aching hardness for her.

He waited though. He waited until she had heard all she needed to and only then did he call her to him.

* * *

The four gathered at breakfast the next morning. Charlotte had set the table outside, with the cushioned garden chairs on the patio. 'Sleep well?' she asked as

David and Anna came outside. 'I think it will be warm today. Do you have sunscreen?'

Anna smiled back and a conversation began about sun factors.

Music Morris Made
Tenille Brown

Vita hadn't always been a homebody. On any given Friday she might be out dancing, or sitting in a lounge somewhere listening to blues or jazz. But it was getting cold in Virginia now, and those were normally things one did with a partner, so, more and more, Vita found herself in bed with warm Kahlua and coffee, clicking the remote control.

It was the season, she guessed. This was the time where folks linked up and cuddled on cold nights. When they watched an old movie and wound up twisted like soft pretzels under the covers, legs locked, body parts clicking together like puzzle pieces.

But Vita had danced that routine for the past six years and she was taking an intermission right now, after she and Darren had called it quits.

Vita was getting used to living alone and she also had found a solution for those nights when it wasn't so cold, when there was all but a raging fire inside her. It came in the form of a three-speed vibrator that she named Roy, and he rested in the drawer, right next to Vita's bed.

Most times, that was enough, but others it was crystal clear to Vita that there were things a vibrator simply couldn't do. It couldn't kiss you, for instance, or hold you after the fucking was done, though Vita wasn't really the spooning type. It couldn't turn you over and fuck you hard, doggy-style. And it certainly didn't have arms and hands with which to smack you soundly on your bottom when you wanted.

And, as if her thoughts were a cue, Vita heard Morris's music start to play upstairs.

As always, it started around 2 a.m. He was like an alarm, except that Morris wasn't the loud, annoying kind. Morris was the rhythmic kind that caused you to wake up smiling. Morris made music.

And maybe he waited so late because Vita should be fast asleep at that hour, having to be at work the next morning and all, but Vita was a night owl, and Morris had no way of knowing that.

Vita was also a light walker, which was probably why she should have been on the top floor instead of him. But, no, Vita was right beneath him, sitting at her kitchen table listening to Morris raise his wide palm high and bring it down hard on his girlfriend Jane's round vanilla ass.

The late-night symphony started about a month ago, shortly after this Jane woman started spending nights over. Vita didn't hear much of their other sexual play, though. She couldn't tell whether Jane preferred being on top or if Morris liked fucking Jane doggy-style. Maybe it was that Vita just didn't pay that part any attention, or it didn't *catch* her attention like the spanking did. But that was because Vita knew that particular sound like, well, the back of her hand. She knew it like her favourite song.

It wasn't like the steady knocking of a headboard against the wall. No, it was much more precise and sharper. And the range would change from time to time. It was eclectic, like a nice cut off a jazz album.

Whether Morris was raising his hand higher or bringing it lower or striking quicker, his notes varied. Whether he was using a strap, a paddle or a whip, the tone would change.

Vita figured that on some nights there was fabric between Morris's palm and Jane's rump. It could be something as thin as a pair of fishnet stockings or as thick and tough as a pair of vinyl pants.

Vita remembered then that, when *she* was getting spanked, she liked it with pants still on. It meant that

Darren had to spank harder to really bring his point home.

Vita leaned back in her chair and listened to the punishment session upstairs. She remembered how it would hurt so good to peel her skin-tight jeans off her reddened ass and pull away her saturated panties when Darren was done.

Darren plunging into her immediately when he was done was the bonus, when the front of his hips pressed firmly against her sore cheeks.

But Vita was digressing and the spanking upstairs was getting louder now and more intense. She sipped her wine and listened to the sound of Morris's drumming hand.

Vita smiled the way she always found herself smiling when Morris was making music. The way she would smile when she saw him the morning after, picking up his paper or checking the mail.

Vita also saw him with Jane some days, too. That meant there was actually a face to match the moans and the feline cries, which made listening to them even more sweetly unbearable.

Jane was pretty. There were no two ways about it. She had bouncy brown hair in a pixie cut and the widest smile, and her ass was plump and taut, and well proportioned to her slender waist. It was hard to hate Jane.

Not that Vita *wanted* to hate her, or even needed to.

Vita was a looker herself, long legs, just enough breasts and naturally curly hair that she kept cropped close. Her fair skin was blemish-free and she hardly wore any makeup. Just a little lipgloss when she remembered to smear some on.

So it was never uncomfortable or disheartening running into Morris with Jane. Many times, Vita just wanted to giggle. She had to bite her tongue when she wanted to say straight to Jane's face, 'I heard you last night, getting spanked.'

Of course, Vita always thought better of it and she found herself saying nothing mostly, a greeting in passing, but nothing so jaw-dropping that it showed on her face that she listened and enjoyed when Morris spanked Jane.

Vita didn't want Jane to think she was envious either, because she wasn't that type, but there were those times when she truly wished that she was the one being punished, that it was her ass that was being spanked.

Sitting at the table, Vita wondered what face Morris might be making now. Morris certainly wasn't bad to look at. In fact, Vita found that she rather liked looking at him, especially when he left for his morning run and his toffee-coloured calves flexed in a sprint.

Jane was certainly a lucky girl.

With the many long nights that Morris had, to get up, take a run and still go off to work, the man had stamina.

But Vita, she had stamina too, and, right now, she

would drink this glass of wine, grab Roy from his resting place and crawl under her covers with him.

Her eyes closed, Vita joined in on the action.

Each strike from Morris's palm to Jane's ass sent a vibration throughout Vita's body, from her nipples to the base of her belly, to her centre where she held Roy at her clit, the strong vibration stimulating her into wetness.

Vita worked her toy slowly at first, wanting to last as long as Morris and Jane did, but she found herself coming before Jane ever did, even before Morris, but that was OK.

It was just what Vita needed, and, for the moment, it was just enough.

* * *

That night was just the beginning of Vita joining in on all the spanking fun. And, honestly, Vita thought it had been a one-time thing. She had foolishly blamed it on the fact that she was restless and just needed some relief of all the tension and it wouldn't happen again.

But it did happen again ... and again.

Every time she heard them above her, it was like a light tap on her shoulder, inviting her to join them. And Vita always accepted the invitation.

Sometimes she used her fingers. Sometimes she used Roy. Sometimes she wore lingerie. Sometimes she was naked, but she always got off.

These days, Vita was embarrassed when she ran into Morris the morning after. It was like taking a walk of shame.

She would keep her head down, mumble 'hello' or something resembling that, and keep on walking.

Then she would come home from work and wait for them at night. He and Jane averaged two, sometimes three sessions a week. It was obvious that one or both of them were fans of spanking. Vita was thankful for that because she was, too.

One morning, though, Vita was unable to avoid him.

She was rather shocked to see Morris approaching her as she walked to her car. Maybe *she* had gotten too loud. Maybe he had heard *her* joining in with their action the night before.

But the look on his face wasn't accusing, it wasn't even devious. Morris was looking quite innocent.

'Morning, neighbour,' he said.

'Morning, Morris,' Vita answered as plainly as she could manage.

'You remember my name?' Morris leaned against her car, which made Vita rather nervous.

'I do,' Vita said, flipping through her keys.

Morris nodded. 'Anyway, I was wondering something. I noticed that on Wednesdays you're usually home during the day.'

'That's my day off.'

'Well, I have the cable guy scheduled to come by tomorrow around noon. 'Cause they can never seem to be able to come after five, you know.'

'I know,' Vita said. And she wished Morris would hurry and get on with it, because her cheeks were becoming flushed just standing there next to him.

'And I would normally get someone else to do it, but Jane will be working and, well, if it wouldn't be too much trouble, I was wondering if you could sit in my apartment for an hour or two while he installs it. Though I'm sure it wouldn't take that long.' He added, 'And there's some beer in the fridge.'

Vita smiled. 'You don't owe me anything.'

'Good. Thank you ... um ...'

'Vita, my name is Vita.'

* * *

Morris left Vita his spare key the next morning, and she used it fifteen minutes before the cable guy arrived. Vita was curious, that was a fact, but she couldn't fully blame her entering his bedroom on curiosity. She mostly wanted to be inside the space, to inhale the scents and imagine the scene.

She was still there when the cable guy knocked on the door, and she returned to it after she let him in and left him to his work in the living room.

He asked, 'This your place?'

And Vita answered, 'No. It's my boyfriend's.'

It wasn't that Vita wanted to claim Morris, but she didn't want to seem like a snoop either.

By that time, she was stretched across his king-sized bed, staring at the wide leather belt hanging on Morris's doorknob. A paddle hung from a nail on the wall, fraternity paraphernalia, but also something Vita knew he used in his punishment.

She stood up and took a short black strap from his dresser and ran it across her palms.

All of it, the room, the implements, made Vita wonder. Was Jane always vocal or did Morris sometimes bind her mouth closed? Did Jane take his cock in her mouth afterwards as a thank-you or were his moans from pressing himself deep inside her?

Maybe Morris liked –

'See something you like?' Morris interrupted her viewing, interrupted her thoughts.

It startled Vita so much that the leather strap fell from her hands to the floor, landing across her shoes. She was almost afraid to turn around, but she had no choice.

Vita cleared her throat. 'Well, the door was open, and I went to close it. I mean, who wants some creepy cable guy nosing through their stuff, you know? But I noticed that, um, you had some ... *stuff* lying about and I just wanted to –'

144

Morris halted Vita's explanation by throwing up both hands. 'No need. I'm not even embarrassed.'

But Vita couldn't say the same. 'I feel terrible about it. I'm really not a snoop. But … sometimes, well, every time actually, I can hear you guys up here.'

'Thin ceilings, eh?' Morris half-flashed his white smile.

'I guess.'

'You never said anything.'

'Well, it doesn't bother me.'

'You sure? I mean, we could keep it down.'

'No, don't … please.'

Vita couldn't believe she was bold enough to say it. Even she didn't know where she got the balls.

Then Morris *really* smiled. And it wasn't a cocky, asshole smile. He actually seemed flattered.

Morris pursed his lips and winked.

* * *

Vita's phone rang, waking her out of a sleep brought on by a boring late-night movie. She clicked her phone on, but, before she could say anything, she heard the sound of heavy breathing.

What Vita wasn't in the mood for just after midnight was a perverse prank call. She was prepared to shout and curse, to really let loose on the son of a bitch who was playing jokes on the phone, but then Vita heard the strike.

At first she couldn't tell if it was coming from upstairs in Morris's apartment or through the phone. But Vita soon realised that it was both.

Morris's phone must have dialled hers somehow. But why her number? And where exactly did he keep his phone, anyway?

There was another strike. It sounded like Morris was using a belt this time, and a heavy one.

'You deserve every bit of this, Jane,' Morris said.

'Yes,' Jane breathed. 'Yes, I know.'

Jane was whimpering close by with painful ecstasy in her voice.

Vita wanted to do the same.

She briefly wrestled with the idea of whether she should hang up or remain on the line. Whether it really was an accident, or if Morris and Jane were extending some sort of invitation.

So, Vita muted her phone and laid it on the pillow next to her. She stripped off her gown and panties and anxiously placed her fingers inside her pussy.

Vita dug deep into herself, moaning.

She was making music herself, except they couldn't exactly hear hers, and, when her melody came to a crescendo, Vita pressed her face into her pillow and screamed.

* * *

It became a regular occurrence, this thing between the three of them. The phone calls came as regularly as the spankings did, came as regularly as Morris, Jane and Vita did.

Vita stayed home on Friday nights for it. She turned down movie dates for it. It had become Vita's new sex life.

She became accustomed to it, never thinking past the moment, never wondering if and when it would end.

But then, one night, Vita was awakened by the silence, and it occurred to her that this was their third silent night in a row.

For a moment, Vita worried that she had slept right through it. She checked her phone for missed calls, but there were none.

Her fingers twitched and itched to dial his number.

But what if Jane *was* there, nestled in the crook of Morris's arm? What if they were sleeping?

Fuck it.

Vita dialled his number.

Morris's voice was groggy and deep, laced with sleep.

Vita said, 'It's been quiet up there lately.'

'She's gone, that's why.'

'Oh, some kind of work thing or something?'

Morris sighed. 'No, she's just gone.It's over.'

And Vita nearly felt like Morris was breaking up with *her*.

She tried to decipher what it was she heard in his voice.

'Are you OK?' she asked, because she didn't know what else would be appropriate.

'I'm fine,' he said. 'It wasn't that serious between us.'

Vita nodded as if Morris could see it.

'I do miss the company, though,' he said matter-of-factly. Then: 'Are you coming?'

* * *

Vita was there, at his door. She didn't change her clothes. She didn't want to make it obvious. It was a simple satin camisole and short set, sexy, but in no way overt.

Morris opened the door bare-chested, wearing plaid pyjama pants. He opened it wide enough for Vita to walk through and then closed it again.

His apartment looked different in the dark of night, sexier, dangerous even, like walking into a dungeon.

Maybe it looked this way because Vita was expecting certain things. Already she could see herself tied to his bedposts, face down on his pillows, being punished.

She lay with her ass toward him, and that was on purpose. His automatic stiffness, Vita imagined, was *not*. It felt nice, but it wasn't the hardness of Morris's cock that Vita craved.

Vita didn't want to be forward, but she already knew they were beyond being coy. She pulled his hand around her waist first and arched her back, rounding her behind more into his crotch. She was aching for the music that he made with his hands, with his paddle, with his whip.

Morris adjusted himself in the bed and lowered his hand down the front of Vita's shorts. His hand was pressing against her panties, then *inside* them.

He was finger-fucking Vita, using the index and middle. After Morris had spent ample time playing in Vita's cunt, once she was getting wet and she was squirming, he then ...

Morris turned Vita over, and then he pulled her back until she was on all fours on his bed.

Vita exhaled. Finally, she was getting what she was waiting for, what she had been desperately craving. He snatched down her shorts and removed her panties in a matter of seconds. And wait ... was that his face between her ass cheeks, his tongue darting in and out?

Yes, Vita liked that, too. She liked the way he plunged in with no hesitation. With his full lips, Morris kissed and sucked the centre of Vita's ass.

'I'm an ass man by the way, in case you couldn't tell,' he said, and laughed.

* * *

It only made it worse when he grabbed her ass, which he did often. Morris grabbed handfuls of her cakes and pulled her close to him, fucking her solidly and silently, filling her with his thick beautiful cock.

149

He gave her all the cock she could stand, but never laid a hand, paddle or whip on her ass.

And *that* was probably what finally made Vita snap.

She got up one night and, instead of spending the night, she left Morris's apartment and returned to her own.

Vita figured she could sleep in her own bed if Morris was simply refusing to give up the goods.

Vita wanted the feel of his hand, scorching hot on her rear end, and he had yet to give it to her, even once, not even a playful slap.

Yes, she was mad at Morris. And she was mad at herself for being mad at him, and being mad about the spanking, or the lack thereof.

So, she made sure to check her mail *after* he had already checked his. She made sure to leave for work only *after* he did. And she didn't linger in the parking lot hoping he'd look down from his balcony and see her, either.

Fuck him.

But then Morris started calling, and Vita ignored that, too. But what she couldn't ignore was the knock on her door just after midnight. Morris was there in his chequered pyjamas, this time with a T-shirt and slippers on too.

'What the fuck is your problem?' he asked her outright.

It stunned Vita a bit and she hesitated. 'Well,' she said, 'to put it simply, you're a fucking tease.'

'But I thought this was what you wanted. What we both wanted.'

'Listen, I know I'm not Jane and I'm not asking you to marry me or anything. I'm just asking for *some* of the same that she got. Not all of it.'

But to come right out and ask Morris for what she really wanted seemed desperate to Vita, so she didn't.

Vita started to close the door, but Morris jammed his foot against it. 'I heard from Jane today. She called.'

Vita was stunned. It felt as if something inside her collapsed. That was it, she supposed. Whatever it was they were doing was on its way down the tubes.

He was going back to Jane, back to spanking her lovely ass. Vita felt the disappointment, though she told herself that couldn't be what she was feeling. She tried not to let it show on her face when she turned around, or come through in her voice when she said, 'Oh yeah? How did that go?'

Morris shrugged. 'She finally decided to tell me the real reason why she wanted it to be over.'

'And why is that?' Though Vita wasn't exactly sure she really wanted to know.

'She found out about you.'

'About me? But me and you, this … this came after.'

'No, she was pissed at the fact that you heard, at the fact that I was letting you listen. She checked my phone one night while I was in the bathroom. She never said anything about it. She just left and didn't come back.'

'I'm sorry, Morris. I'm so sorry,' Vita said.

'It's not your fault. I didn't have to call you all those nights.'

'Still …'

'Yeah, I know.' Morris shrugged. 'Shit happens, I guess. We were doomed anyway. Our schedules were crazy.'

But the more Vita thought about it, the more she wondered how big a role she *did* play in the break-up, and she wondered what she could do to make it right.

'I'll tell you what. You can blame it on me, Morris.'

'Vita, I don't want to blame it on you. I don't want to blame it on anyone.'

'No, Morris. You don't get what I'm saying. Whatever anger or frustration you might be feeling about this situation, just take it out on me.'

'Take it out on you?'

'Yes,' Vita said, 'me and my ass.'

And Morris's full lips turned up into a sly smile.

* * *

Morris was punishing Vita so rapidly and so hard with the wooden ruler she almost wanted to apologise. But she endured the pain, enjoyed the hot, sharp sensation on her skin, biting on her bottom lip when she wasn't begging him not to stop.

'I want to see burgundy,' Morris said, out of breath from the relentless striking.

Strike.

Vita threw her head back, curls grazing her shoulder blades.

'And I want it to sting for hours,' Vita said, clenching the sheets between her eager fingers.

Strike.

'Happy to oblige,' Morris said.

He dropped the ruler on the bed, and began using his hand.

Strike.

* * *

It was his technique, Vita decided, that made Morris so good at what he did. And the fact that he was unpredictable. She never knew when it was coming, though Morris never made her wait too long.

He would call and she would come, strip down and climb on to the bed, ass to him. Sometimes he would bind her wrists and press her against the wall while he used a paddle.

His tempo was wildly out of sorts, yet right on target. The sounds, up close and personal, were ever melodic, as were the thrashings.

Vita was sore, always so sweetly sore afterwards, but never in too much pain not to come whenever he called.

Vita had replaced Jane, and she was fine with that, but she imagined that maybe one day someone would replace *her*.

Then again, maybe not. Maybe the universe placed her here, exactly here, with Morris under the plentiful sting of his magical palm.

And as Morris laid another wonderful strike, Vita noticed Morris's phone lit up on the nightstand. Turning her head slightly, she didn't recognise the number, but she certainly knew the name.

It was Jane.

Vita's lips slowly parted in a merging of shock and satisfaction.

She could stop Morris mid-strike, stop him right here, right now. It could be that simple, if Vita wanted it to be.

But instead, Vita said, 'Morris, spank me harder,' and folded Morris's phone closed.

New Dress
Charlotte Stein

I know I've said the wrong thing when everything goes deathly silent behind the bathroom door. But really, I can't be blamed, can I? I mean, surely anyone else would have done the same thing, in my position. It sounded like he'd fallen down and seriously injured himself in there. It sounded like someone had snuck in through the bathroom window and decided to kill him.

But now that everything's quiet, and thrumming with a kind of mortification, I know that's not the case. Those sounds I heard, of flesh hitting flesh and then the gasps and strange cries.

Yeah. He was doing something sexual in there.

A fool would know it, but apparently I'm a fool because I didn't know. And now I'm just frozen to the spot outside the bathroom door, breathlessly anticipating his next move. Is he going to try to hedge it, and act as though nothing was going on? Laugh it off, and bluster his way out of there with his head held high?

He's not really that sort of guy, but I can imagine him at least trying.

So it's a shock when he doesn't. In answer to my little ridiculous query – 'Are you OK in there, Brad?' – he just puts it right out there. 'No,' he says. 'No, I need to finish. Can you give me a second?'

All I can think is: dear God, finish *what*? Because I swear, if he's jerking off in there, it's the most violent masturbation session in the history of masturbation sessions. He's in serious danger of amputating something if he carries on that way, but then ... maybe he's not doing anything like that.

'Finish' could mean anything. Could be that he's in there doing some latest exercise craze, and if he doesn't do all four hundred reps he's going to lose that amazing muscle definition he so often flaunts about the house. There I am, reading my morning paper, and there he is, half-naked across the dining table we share, pyjama bottoms slung way too low on his solid hips.

Everything about him screaming, *Come for it, then*.

But I never do come for it, because what if I'm wrong? He's just my flatmate. My strange, goofy and utterly handsome flatmate, who is currently in the bathroom, finishing a thousand sink pull-ups.

'OK, well, I'll just be in the living room,' I say, which seems like a reasonable thing to go with. Or at least it does, until I consider another rather troubling possibility. One that sounds stupid coming out, but needs to be voiced anyway. 'You're not doing anything bad in there, are you?'

Of course, I'm thinking of some pretty serious stuff. Razorblades cutting into his milk-pale skin, rivulets of blood running dark and red into the sink. Those little sounds bursting out of him whenever he slices a little too deep, and skirts close to the emergency room.

I mean, *I'm* the one who'll have to get him off the bathroom floor and drag him out. And though I have total faith in my ambulance-calling abilities, I'm not so sure if I have enough upper-body strength to get him into some sort of recovery position. He's the size of a bus.

A bus who then replies, 'What do you mean by bad?'

And though the words aren't exactly inflammatory, there's definitely something about his tone. Something I can't place. Something far away and yet so close at the same time, like a hummingbird buzzing between us. Reach out for it, and it flits away.

'I mean ... you know. You're not hurting yourself, are you?'

Again, there's this pause. One that I suppose sounds like it means something more, even though I don't know what that something more is. It feels practised, that pause. It feels pregnant, despite the fact that I've never really thought a pause could actually be filled with gestating children.

'No,' he says, after a while.

But it sounds like he's *lying*.

'Because you know, if you were, that's OK. And you can talk to me about it, if you need to.'

Another long, long pause. This one seems filled with more than babies.

'You want me to talk about this?'

He sounds incredulous. Like I just suggested he poke a hole in himself and let all of his guts spill out. Though, when I really think about it, that's kind of what I have done. I've invited him to share something with me – something I don't think I'm going to be prepared for.

'Yeah. Why not? That's what friends are for, right?'

I honestly don't think they're for this, but hey. I'm knee-deep in his secrets now. I might as well continue into the swamp, to see what turns up. I mean, he's a good guy. He deserves that much from me.

'I guess. Though I don't think you're really going to want to hear about this.'

My mind tries to go to a million weird things he could possibly be doing, but none of them seems possible.

Instead, I'm just left with a pounding heart and this odd watery feeling running through me, as though a year of patient friendship with the guy behind the door has been leading to this ... whatever this is.

'Try me,' I say, and then I hold my breath. He's not really going to do it, is he? It's entirely possible he won't. It was only yesterday I found out that he has a brother and used to live in Maryland – it's unlikely that he's going to share intimate secrets through a bathroom door.

'Maybe you should just come in, and see.'

Well, I guess I was right on that front. He doesn't want to share through a bathroom door. He wants me to come in, and for a moment I can't. My heart has started pounding in my eyeballs. Those weird possibilities are beginning to take on some sort of form and shape in my mind, though things still aren't exactly as I expect when I finally get the door open.

He has his pants tugged down, for a start. And, although I know that should seem silly, somehow, there's something about the sight of him like that ... something I don't quite anticipate. He looks rude, I think, rude and bad and filthy, trousers yanked to mid-thigh as though some mysterious intruder did it to him.

And his flesh seems just so ... exposed. At the best of times he's the colour of a January sky, but right here and now his skin seems almost tenderly pale. I can see a thin tracery of veins here and there, faint and yet somehow vivid at the same time, and when he turns a little there's something almost hypnotic about the muscles shifting in his thighs.

For a second, I think I forgot he's a big guy. But now that I'm really staring I can't help but uncover a variety of little pleasures. Like the solid line of his legs, as they slide up into the curve of his ass. The hint of muscle twisting just above the line of his pubic hair and ... *oh my God, I'm looking at his pubic hair.*

Those dark curls – they're ... you know. His rude parts. And they get ruder the further down you go, because he's not really trying to show what's between his legs but he's not really trying to hide it, either. I glance up at his face, briefly, and he just looks bashful and sort of mildly embarrassed, like maybe he wants me to look but isn't sure how to properly go about it.

Properly is dates and holding hands and do-you-want-to-come-ups. It isn't this, and he obviously knows it.

But I'm looking at his stiff cock, anyway. Because of course he's stiff. How could he not be? He's doing something rude in the bathroom and I just caught him, and now I'm stood here staring at him with a probably heated gaze.

I mean, I'm pretty sure I don't look horrified by this. I can't look horrified, because his cock is thick and curving and delicious, and at the tip I can see a lazy strand of fluid easing its way down, down over his shaft.

I can't deny it. There's something almost unbearably arousing about that. It makes me think of words like *shameless* and *whore*, though God only knows who I'm applying them to. I mean, I'm swollen between my legs and far wetter than he is, but he doesn't know it. I'm not yet worthy of a label as thrilling as *slut*.

But he is.

He looks like a slut. A bad, bad slut.

'Are you disgusted?' he asks, and my instinct is to say the strangest thing. I don't find him disgusting – not in the slightest – and he's so sweet that telling him something like that would probably hurt me in the same way that punching a kitten might. And yet, I kind of want to say it anyway.

Yeah. Yeah, you're disgusting, you little trollop.

'No,' I say, but it doesn't sound as sure as I'd like it to. And when he turns just a little bit more, when he lets me see the curve of his ass more fully, I can't stop my gasp escaping. I sound like a swooning maiden and he's bound to think he really is being gross, but it's just impossible to stop.

Because he hasn't just been jerking off in here. He's been … hurting himself. Spanking himself, I guess, though the stark red marks on his flesh look like more than handprints. They're so dark they're almost bloody, burning hot close to the centre and then edging out into fans of mottled pink. In some places, I can see where the smacks have overlapped, lines almost like ridges crossing fainter ones – as though he had to up the stakes on every strike.

And weirdly it's this thought that makes me go all funny inside. He had to keep striving for harder, because a faint little love tap wasn't enough. He needed more than that, craved more than that, and now this is the result.

Him with his cock all swollen and rampant. Me with my nipples poking stiffly through the T-shirt I'm wearing.

'Are you disgusted now?' he asks, though I can't for the life of me think what's changed. Does he imagine that the stripes on his ass are going to be the thing that pushes me over the edge? I hate to disappoint him, but … I can't say that's the reaction I'm having.

Instead, I think something intensely strange: *the red looks so beautiful against the white.* And those words, buzzing around my head and infiltrating things they shouldn't, they make me want to ask a question.

One that has no bearing on our relationship to date.

'How did you make marks like that?'

He glances at me – checking for evidence of disapproval, I think. But I don't think it's disapproval on my face. It feels like something else, something that's sort of like telling someone off but maybe not in any real way.

Maybe it's more like a fantasy sort of way. You know, like when you play at being Batman as a kid, only, when you apprehend your friend who's dressed up as the Joker, you're not *really* apprehending him.

You're just sort of playing along. Slipping into a role. And, oh, this role feels like fine silk against my skin. It feels like a dress I've been wearing all my life, only it's so sheer I can't even see it when I look in the mirror.

'I ... uh ...' he starts, but I can't let him carry on like that. He sounds pathetic and weak and small, and it's simply not good enough.

'Tell me,' I say, and, although I don't think I make my voice any different, something definitely happens to him when I do. His shoulders go back, his lips part. A new look comes into his eyes – one that I sort of recognise, but, oh God, not really.

Oh, Lord, what am I doing?

'I use this,' he says, and then he shows me the little paddle in his hand.

Of course, I have a very limited experience of stuff like that. I wouldn't know one sex toy from another. But I understand this much: it has holes in it, which will almost certainly give a more painful blow. And it's quite thin, too, so I imagine it stings when it hits.

But, oh, he can't possibly be getting a good swing on it. I think he's making the marks by continually catching himself with the end of it, or maybe alternating between the paddle and one of his broad hands. But, of course, unless I see it for myself I've got no idea at all.

'Show me,' I say, and for a second he balks. His face reddens to the colour of his ass, and he plucks at the thing in his hand nervously. But then I settle my gaze on him – one that I intend as a kind of reminder of what I've already seen. Because, really, what does it matter now?

But the thing is – I think it comes out harder than that. I think I feel cold, suddenly, behind my eyes. Like I should brook no refusal, even though I hardly know what something like that means.

And then he obeys, just like that. He kind of turns his head and won't look at me, before bringing the paddle down so suddenly and so dexterously I almost miss it. Clearly, he's done this a million times before. He doesn't even let out a gasp this time, though I'm sure it must have hurt.

Which just makes me wonder about all of those gasps I heard behind the bathroom door, and how quiet he was really trying to be. I mean, it's not as though I went far. I only called at the shops and he should have known I'd be returning any second. But he let me hear him anyway, making sounds he clearly doesn't when he thinks things are more private.

'This is really shocking behaviour, Brad,' I say, and am stunned by how stern my voice is. It's so stern, in fact, that he babbles in response.

'Oh, God, I'm sorry, I'm sorry – I don't mean to do

164

it but I just *have* to, I *need* it. Work is so stressful at the moment and –'

'Don't make excuses,' I say, like a hand rapping on a door. And even more remarkably, he falls immediately silent. Eyes still trained on something other than me. That paddle gripped sweatily in one fist. 'Just admit it – you've always done this, haven't you? It has nothing to do with work.'

I don't know how I dare. I've certainly got no real idea if what I'm saying is true or not. And yet I want to, I want to, I *need* to say those words to him.

'Yes,' he replies – sullenly, I think.

His dark hair has fallen into his eyes and his mouth looks soft and sulky, and, oh, God, I don't think I can take much more of him. He smells like cinnamon and apples, and he's all raw and obviously aroused and I'm talking like this, I'm talking and talking and I don't know who I am anymore.

'Bend over the sink, Brad,' I say, and, oh, how he moans in response. He moans and squirms and it's as though every one of those little reactions connect directly to my clit. Any second he's going to say something whiny like *please no, I don't want to*, and, oh, dear Lord, I'm going to *love* it.

'Bend over, and give me the paddle,' I tell him again, in a colder voice.

And this time he obeys. He just hands it over to me,

body violently trembling as he does so, those black-as-midnight eyes of his suddenly shut tight.

'You've been bad,' I tell him, which I'm sure is probably the hokiest thing a person can say in this situation. It's a cliché right from the BDSM handbook, page one, paragraph one, line one.

But then, that's where I'm at. I'm on the Beginner's Pamphlet, still waiting to find out if the rules suit me. Because there are rules, aren't there? I mean, I'm not supposed to really hurt him. Or what if that's not the rule at all – maybe I *am* supposed to really hurt him. Maybe he wants me to reduce him to a blubbering, twitching mess on the bathroom floor, unable to sit down the next day without a reminder of me burning up through his body.

Is that the way it works?

'Hold still, Brad,' I say, and then I crack that thing down on him so hard.

Or at least, I think I do it hard. It certainly seems as though I do when I feel it whooshing through the air, and then the heavy connection of it with his gorgeous flesh. That connection spreads from him and back into me, all the way up my arm and into some heretofore undiscovered centres of my brain, most of which sizzle and spark and say things to me like: *Slip a hand into your panties. Just slip a hand in and stroke your clit, while you spank him.*

But I resist. I resist right up until the point where he says some sort of glorious, insane, magical word: 'Harder.'

God, I thought I *did* do it hard. I can already see the mark I've made, tugging the pink of his ass back to a glorious crimson. But apparently, in the world of Brad Henderson and his thirst for corporal punishment, I'm just a wussy.

'Like this?' I ask, and this time I bring it down heavily. Not like a spank. More like a *thud*, a heavy dull thud on his perfect ass – one that makes my shoulder ache and my body judder under its pressure, as though I'm hurting myself as much as I'm hurting him.

I think I almost make the same sound he does, when it connects. A sob, thick and breathless but buried under the press of my lips.

Of course, he doesn't try to bury his. He lets it out, so loud it reverberates around the bathroom and all the way through me. It spurs me to test out this newfound power, slapping him hard and fast with just the very edge of it, then slow and softer and heavier.

Both seem to make him shudder, but the ones that connect more solidly provoke a slightly different reaction. A lower note to his gasps, a hint of words in among all of them. And when I lean in close I can almost hear what he's trying to say – a little fluttering of pleases and yeses and mores.

I think it's the sound of those exhortations that finally pushes me to do something about the hot throb that's taken over my body. Of course, I have to do it when he isn't looking, but that's not all that hard considering he hasn't so much as glanced at me since all of this began.

His shoulders are hunched and I can see that his hand has disappeared to some place in front of him, so it doesn't seem like I'm doing the wrong thing by sliding my fingers under the waistband of my skirt. Even though it completely feels like the wrong thing once I've done it. It feels like the dirtiest thing in the world, and the pressure of the material against the back of my hand doesn't make it any better.

But it does make it *hotter*. I can hardly reach, and my other arm is aching from the swinging I can't seem to stop, but the moment I get close ...

My body thrills before I've even found and rubbed over my clit. Just the feel of my soaked panties, and the swollen curve of my outer lips standing out so stark through the material ... it's enough to make me miss the next spank.

I think I catch him on the backs of his thighs somewhere, but he doesn't seem to mind. He's groaning now, really groaning, and, beneath the steady, flat rhythm of the paddle hitting his flesh, I can make out another, slicker one.

He's jerking off, while I mark him and masturbate to the sound of his voice.

'Oh, God, yeah, just like that,' he tells me, and I don't know what's more blissful about it. That he's so desperate when he blurts out the words, or that I now know I'm doing it exactly right. Somehow I've hit upon the perfect pace, the perfect ferocity, and after a second of striping him almost black and blue with my little paddle he lets out this glorious sound – all long and drawn out and so thick with lust.

It's like nothing I've ever heard before, and I don't mind admitting that it sends a rush of pleasure down through my body. I'm still barely touching my clit, fingers rubbing in some fumbling way at the edges of my sex, but I think I'm going to climax anyway.

I can smell the sharp tang of his come in the air, and when I let the paddle clatter out of my hand it's all I can do not to grab him. There's so much I want to feel and lick and touch – the streaks of perspiration on his back, where his shirt's riled up. The mess he's obviously made of himself, somewhere just out of reach.

And most of all those marks, those searing red marks. I can almost feel the heat radiating off them the second I lean in, and, though I know I shouldn't find it so, his wince when I press against him is *exquisite*.

It makes me think of him clenching his teeth, tensing his fists, biting down hard. And all of these things push me until I'm suddenly beneath the wet material of my panties, stroking over everything that isn't my clit.

If I touch myself there, I know I'll die. At the very least, I won't ever be able to go back. Bad enough that I spanked my roommate until he came all over his fist. Masturbating with the thought of that bright, brilliant pain in my head is a step too far. Anyone would know it.

But as usual, I don't.

'Go on,' he says. 'Come all over me. Get yourself off.'

How strange that this is the first time I've ever heard him say something truly dirty. But, oh, how sweet it is, how like the same sort of permission I gave him only moments before. I arch against him to hear it, just one finger stroking through my slick slit until I find that swollen little bead.

And then I give in; I give in and rub over it with my face pressed to his still heaving back, that heat pouring through me and under me and over me. My orgasm is so fierce it feels like pain, like someone striking hard on my exposed flesh, and when I call something out it isn't his name.

'Thank you,' I tell him instead, though I don't know what I'm thanking him for. Didn't I give him something, after all? Didn't I hurt him in just the way he wanted, and needed, and so desperately longed for?

I guess I did, and yet I'm the one sobbing into his back. My legs won't hold me up, the pleasure won't stop pulsing from that single point beneath my working finger, and it's in this moment that I realise what *he* has given *me*.

A new dress, I think. A new dress, made of silk. And, oh, it's perfect.

Spite
Ashley Hind

Her name comes from Irish Gaelic and translates variously as *lightness and radiance*, *bright and shining*, or *little bright one*. None of these quite encapsulates just how much she shone on me. She was more to me than the sun, but even in the earliest days I knew if I was not careful then I would get burned. Sorcha was my first love, my only love. I was a simple girl, pretty but unrefined, a little coarse even. But she polished my dull roughness and made me shine like her. She filled me to bursting with all the beauty of the world: laughter and song, poetry and shared secrets, hot longing on silver beaches and warm kisses on crisp winter mornings. And then she left me.

So all the poetry is gone and I am empty once more. The joy has turned to bitterness and left only the gnawing desire to make her hurt like I do. My spite consumes me. I want to chip and then shatter her with revenge, the effects of which I will never see and which will never be enough to sate me. Even the defeat I have inflicted this night, the one she is about to walk headlong into, even this is not enough; it is merely the start. I am not discouraged by the hollowness of my victory, or that it might provoke her vengeance. Any retribution from her will only feed my sense of injustice and make my cause stronger. I will go on and on, relentless in my path of destruction, until some other girl comes to put out the fire in my wronged soul, and makes me love again the way Sorcha once did.

* * *

I fell for the ethereal perfection of her looks and her surprising strength and spirit. She seemed so different to me. She was so wise and informed, so correct yet spontaneous and wild, so *natural*. In contrast, I am common. I don't lack intelligence but I speak with a lazy North London drawl, and next to her I sound and feel like an imbecile. I am good-looking but wear too much makeup, preferring the heavy goth look to match my short jet-black hair. We are both feminine but, while she seems pure and wholesome, I look and dress like a cross somewhere between a student and a tart. In the beginning I loved the contrast between us. By the time I had realised we were like peas in a pod, I was already way too deep in her, and I elected to flounder rather than attempt to resurface. I would rather have drowned in her than float aimless and alone.

Our similarity lies in our desire to dominate. We both have strong personalities that we like to assert on others. We are happier with our hand on the tiller. While that meant we were decisive and admiring of each other's fortitude, it also ensured conflict came quickly when our opinions were divided. I guess I was more smitten than she, since it was invariably me that gave quarter. That suited her just fine. She was into total obedience, particularly when it came to sex. Really, she wanted a slave to act on her every word. Clearly, this was not me.

Most of all she wanted a girl to worship her feet, a preference I found odd in someone who was otherwise almost obsessively clean. Her toes were her most sensitive place, and she thought that making a girl suck them for her was the ultimate act of subjugation. In contrast, I am just a dirty fucker. I wanted rough, hard, messy sex, the filthier the better. I have stuck dildos in girls' holes and then had them lick them clean. I have spanked bottoms, tits and pussies. I have made girls wet themselves and then gagged them with their own knickers while I stuffed them from behind. I like to be in control because that way I can free my mind and dictate the dirtiness.

The thought of doing anything like that to Sorcha was laughable. She knew my passion to spank and told me in no uncertain terms that she hated to either give or receive pain. She said we would have to part if I could not live with that. Her chosen method of torture and humiliation was by denial. Her ex-girlfriends would be put through a series of menial tasks, none of which was apparently sexual, although both parties seemed to take their own pleasure from it. She could resist almost indefinitely, making them do her bidding for hours, sometimes days, before she relented and release was granted. My lust had no patience. I wanted to burst upon my girls and devour them completely.

One time we were eating in the café of my favourite department store in town. I whispered to Sorcha that I was dying for her to fuck me and that my knickers were soaked. She called me a filthy whore and sent me to the toilet to take them off. She then had me go down the escalator to the lingerie department and hand my soiled panties to the counter assistant, telling her that I had found them in the changing rooms. The look on the assistant's face as the damp crotch of my knickers touched her held-out palm is still vivid. For Sorcha, it wasn't about the rudeness of the action, it was about the fact that I purchased all my sexy underwear there, and after that humiliation I would find it very hard to do so again.

Despite our obvious incompatibility, our sex life was

still intense. I find her so beautiful and alluring that every expression on her face, every move she made or phrase that she uttered turned me on. And when I am turned on I am like an inferno. I want to consume softness, to hurt, to engorge flesh or turn it red. I used to lie beneath her like a smouldering powder keg, reined in by the constant threat of her imminent departure if I exploded on to her, burning inside as she stroked and teased me. I would thrash and yell with the huge release as I was finally able to come on her fingers or on to the toys that frustration had driven me to thrust inside myself while she lay with a smile of mocking contentment beside me.

A couple of times we seduced a third party to see if a new girl could satisfy our differing desires, but the trysts were uncomfortable and only served to highlight the contrasts between us. On the last occasion, while our chosen girl was feasting at Sorcha's feet, I managed to contain my urge to spank the bent-over arse before me and instead pushed my middle finger up the girl's tight bottom and gently fucked her with it. I remember my lover's look of disgust as my filthy lusts poured out on to our victim. I recall, when it was time for the girl to leave, my lover actually apologised to her for my dirtiness.

It began to slip away because neither of us had it within our character to give in. It only went on as long as it did because I loved her more than she loved me and was willing to yield some ground. Sometimes I let her restrain me on the bed for hours, desperate to lick her as she squatted above me, just out of the reach of my tongue as her sex smell poured into my nostrils, or dying to pee as she brushed a peacock feather over my clit and commanded me not to spill a drop unless I wanted to stay bound and teased for further countless hours. Sometimes I even sucked on her toes, but I made it part of our sex play and not an act of reverence. As much as I loved her, I resented having to give in to her when she utterly refused to do the same for me. She knew I did this act grudgingly. I deliberately made it lascivious, rather than either tender and loving, or demeaning. Moreover, she knew it didn't turn me on enough to make me want or *have* to do it again. I could never worship her feet in the way she wanted. And so she found a girl who would.

* * *

I was unceremoniously told that she had found someone else, and that was that. I was so stunned I didn't cry or argue. I just left her there, ghosting from the bar as she went to get more drinks, hiding numbed and bereft in my flat for days and refusing to answer the phone. Two weeks later, ire drove me from my bed and I started to watch her, to find out exactly who had taken my place in her affections. The new flame, the foot-loving submissive bitch that had ripped my world apart, turned out to be a rather unassuming nineteen-year-old called Kerry. She did studenty things by day and worked a few hours in a chip shop most evenings.

Kerry was too sweet-looking to be hateable, too plain to really be considered pretty. The only similarity we shared was our dark hair, hers longer than mine and tied back beneath the cap of her work uniform. She wore no makeup, perhaps because her employers didn't allow it. While her eyes had just enough darkness to remain bold, her lips were pale pink and melted indistinguishably into her face, and you had to study more diligently to realise that they were actually full and appealingly soft-looking. When she smiled, they slowly peeled away to reveal perfect white teeth, and then your eye was drawn up to the dimple in the corner of one cheek. She was a little plump, with a small roll gathering at her belly above her waistline. Her bottom pushed out amply against her black leggings – tempting, infinitely spankable, and completely wasted on her new mistress.

Sorcha would usually come and collect her new girl-friend from work, parking in the spaces behind the shopping parade and hovering about outside to avoid being too obvious. They would wait until they got into the car before they would kiss. On Wednesday nights, Sorcha had her reiki classes and would arrive slightly later. Kerry would be waiting for her, sitting on the low secluded wall at the rear of the car park, clutching a tight white package that contained their fish supper. When Sorcha arrived, they would sit together and eat, right there on the wall, the younger girl smiling and giggling at every word the angel beside her whispered, just like I used to do.

It is odd spying on a couple who think they are safe within the comfort of their own company. It is disconcerting to see their body language of love when you know that yours is crying out to receive it. Although I raged with jealousy, I came to know and recognise their rites and procedures, feeling almost warmth at the familiarity of it all. One time, I even caught myself smiling as I skulked in the shadows, mirroring Kerry's post-kiss look of pleasure that she unfailingly bestowed upon her mistress.

Of course, they never knew I was watching them, and only once did I suspect differently. On one warm, still evening, their supper having been consumed from the package on their knees, Sorcha glanced around her to check on their seclusion and then slipped off her sandal. She leaned forward and whispered her instruction. Kerry duly but apprehensively obeyed, sinking to her knees at the feet of her mistress and lovingly taking her toes into her mouth, one after another, kissing and licking each with tender adoration. It was a clear reminder if any were needed of why she was there and I was not. My ears hissed and my insides fell away as I witnessed her giving what I never could. I collapsed to my knees as Sorcha bent and gave the word, and the two of them skipped merrily back to the car, horny as hell and rushing home to do whatever it was they did when alone.

* * *

It was natural for me to want to get a closer look at my usurper and so I took to visiting the chip shop too. There was no spontaneity to this. I had planned my visits precisely, and adapted them each time to better my chance of success. I went on a Wednesday evening when I knew Sorcha would be otherwise occupied. I got myself pedicures, making sure my toes always looked good enough to eat. I wore open shoes and short skirts to best show myself off. I ignored the other counter assistant and gave Kerry a big welcoming smile. The first visit was brief, but gave me just long enough to let her catch me looking at her a couple of times, and snatching a sideways glance at her bottom. I also learned, courtesy of another customer, to choose scampi and not fish, as it was always cooked to order and this ensured I could be in the shop for longer.

I went after the teatime rush to ensure there would be fewer customers, and this afforded more opportunity for me to talk with her. Our short interchanges blossomed into longer, light-hearted conversations. I made sure I was suggestive and took delight as she giggled and blushed at the rude asides I conspiratorially shared with her alone. I always gave her lots of smiles and eye contact, and let her see me glancing with lustful looks at her chest or bottom when she thought I thought she wasn't looking. By my fourth or fifth visit, it was obvious that I fancied her, and, in case it wasn't, I started greeting her with the phrase 'So how's my pretty girl today, then?'

I made sure I never got on to the subject of her personal relationships, not just because it might have embarrassed her, but also because I wanted Sorcha totally forgotten while Kerry was in my presence. When I sensed her greeting my arrival with a little rush of pleasure, I knew I was ready to begin my endgame.

On maybe my eighth or ninth visit, she was serving alone at the counter, and as I was the only customer waiting I made sure my talk was extra bawdy and my looks even more obviously lustful. That night I bucked my usual trend and asked for a gherkin along with my scampi and chips. She took one out and held it up for my approval, then nearly dropped it as I casually said, 'It's for my girlfriend. She has been very naughty so I'm going to make her put it inside her. After that, I'm going to have her get down and suck my toes. Do you think she will like them?'

Poor Kerry nearly choked. She was speechless, blushing furiously as she tried to hasten her wrapping of my food.

However, I noticed her taking her chance to have a longer look at my feet, and heard her squeak an almost imperceptible answer of 'yes'. I left with a happy heart, and the certain knowledge that she was now ripe for the picking. Pity the poor submissive, they have no power to resist a determined effort to ensnare them – it is in their nature to be seduced. I didn't dwell on the fact that Kerry was perhaps an innocent bystander in all of this and that she was a very amiable girl that I would only normally seek to hurt in a sexual way, not emotionally. I had to force from my mind the nagging fact that I rather fancied her, plain or not, and I could easily see why Sorcha had fallen for her. They were clearly made for each other.

* * *

My *coup de grâce*, performed this very night, was easily achieved and relied on nothing more than the dependability of human nature. Sorcha was at her reiki class. For once I did not go to the shop around eight, but instead watched Kerry through the glass from over the road. I could feel the rise of heart-quickening glee as she glanced up at the clock on the wall above her, checking the time – not once or twice, but three or four times in quick succession. Was she wondering why I hadn't come in as usual? Was she missing me?

At five minutes to nine, just as Sorcha's class was set

to end, I texted my ex-lover, giving her no time to reply or even think about the message, which said: 'Please come. I need help and only you can give it to me. I ask only ten minutes of your time. I am at Latimer's bar.'

I knew it would take ten minutes for her to get there, five to search and not find me, a couple more to text me and then decide to leave, and about ten to get back here. That was all the time I needed. I saw Kerry portioning up their supper in readiness to leave. She came out into the dusk and I watched from the cover of my car as she sat on the low wall, their supper balanced on her knee, tightly bound to retain its warmth.

I went over and sat next to her. Her look flashed surprise, gladness and trepidation all at once. She had been safe from my flirting advances inside the shop, but now she was alone and vulnerable. She smiled and stammered, 'I'm waiting for someone.'

Doubtless she was hoping this would deter whatever I had in mind for her.

'You are waiting for me,' I said. 'Sorcha has given you to me for the evening. Your mistress wishes you to do my bidding tonight. It is a test, to see if you will obey her commands even when she is not there to give them. She wants to know if you are worthy of her or if she must find another. Do you understand?'

'I'm not sure I should,' she stammered, biting her lower lip, 'I –'

182

'Has she not just texted you to let you know she will be later than normal? This is the reason.'

She was wide-eyed and hesitant but eventually nodded her agreement, since servility is all she will ever know.

'Good,' I said. 'Kiss me then.'

I kissed her gently enough, careful not to scare her off, feeling her soft warm lips dissolve into mine.

'Shall we eat?' I whispered, close to her still.

I took her to my car and perhaps she was glad of its relative privacy in comparison to the wall they usually sat on, and the public show her girlfriend demanded of her. We sat side by side on the back seat and began to eat the food. I kissed her between bites with mounting passion, pulling up her shirt and freeing her little ripe tits from her bra. She smelled of chip fat and perfume, and somehow of youth and innocence. I sucked and nipped her nipples with my teeth, making her gasp. I continued to feed, my fingers slick with chip grease and my own saliva as I pushed them into my mouth. I pulled down her leggings and slid my hand into her knickers to feel her soft mound and its damp waiting split. I rubbed her and made her whimper, feeling her lean into me with an urgency for my firm touch. I plunged my finger into her tight confines and stirred it around the hot pool within. I kissed with even greater hunger, breaking off to take mouthfuls of food as if the feast was part of our passion. I tore off lumps of fish and crammed them in, pulling her to me and making her take her share, smearing her lips with the grease from the batter, having her eat almost from my mouth. The car interior was filled with the smell of food and our urgent longing.

I put her over my knees, the remainder of our meal resting on her back on open paper. I roughly pulled her white cotton panties down and purred at the sight of her luscious arse. I ate and intermittently slid my finger into her, then spanked her bottom a few times as a warning to cease her wriggling. Then my rudeness took over and I pushed a chip up inside her, then another, wiping my greasy come-wet fingers up the crack of her arse between helpings. I took more and forced my fingers within her to deposit the food, feeling the chips break inside from my rough fingering, their floury centres giving a puff of their residual heat as the skin broke.

When I had filled her pussy with chips, I spanked her in earnest. I slapped both her arse cheeks hard, while she yelled out and tried to escape. I could feel the wetness oozing from her and pooling on to my bare thighs. I had forgotten just how blissful it was to spank a really lovely, plump backside. Her delectable jelly of a bottom was making my heart rush with desire and I knew I could easily fall in love with this girl. Each smack pushed her hard against my thighs but, as my hand came back away, she pushed her bum up again, involuntarily willing each new searing contact.

She sobbed, her face crimson and traced with tears, her mouth open as the saliva escaped in threads. I kept beating her young rump until I could feel the heat coming from it, until her squeals had turned to a long low moan and her bucking had become a grinding thrust against my legs. For all the pain and humiliation, she was ready to come. I took the last piece of battered fish and crushed it on to her bottom, spanking it in so that it squashed against her scarlet skin. My fingers were slick with the batter grease and I pulled her cheeks apart and saw her tiny hole above her glistening gash.

I pushed my middle finger up her twitching arse. She gasped and bucked but her anus was too slippery with grease to resist me. I pushed it all the way up and then forced my forefinger in alongside it, stretching her virgin passage open and feeling it clench and squeeze upon me. I very slowly withdrew them both, nearly all the way out of her, right until her little ring was closing in defence against my fingertips. Then in one move I slid them all the way back up again. She squealed and it was gorgeous. I patiently built my rhythm, allowing her time to open and relax, to add her own juices to the chip oil smearing her innards. I knew that the shock of being taken so rudely would not abate, that the humiliation would only grow to scintillating levels as it became obvious to us both how much she was loving this dirty fuck. The visible side of her face showed a rosy red cheek, a closed eye and an open wet mouth. She was lost in the moment and all mine. It almost made me come. In the end, my hand was slapping against her and I was frigging her mercilessly. Her little quim was sending gushes of warm stickiness on to my lap as she wriggled and ground herself against me. She just about managed to stifle a scream and then she was coming, very hard, against my leg.

It was beautiful to have her climax with such intensity but I gave no outward sign of my delight. I showed her no emotional closeness at all, forcing her into action before she even had time to recuperate. I tersely told her to pull up her knickers and leggings. She scrambled from my lap and tried to kiss me but I held her off. Even though I could see that her head was spinning, I simply ordered her to get out of the car and go back over to the wall to sit and await her mistress.

That is how I left her and that is exactly how Sorcha will very soon find her possession, innocently waiting to tell the tale that must surely doom their relationship. The young slave will already be aching for more rough pleasures, unaware as yet that her mistress is incapable of providing them. Sorcha, the once brightness of my life, will get her turn to have her heart ripped out. Each single word will be like a hammer blow as Kerry relates the story of her defilement while still wet and trembling from its effects, and erroneously proud of having done her lover's bidding. And as the story unfolds it will become obvious how I took my vengeful pleasure, how I laid my perverted spite upon the young girl and made her scream and shake with ecstasy. How I left her tainted for ever in her mistress's eyes but never to mine, branded by my filthy touch, her newly plundered arse red, sore and greasy, and her cunt still stuffed full of chips.

Iced Buns
Elizabeth Coldwell

Lena pours icing sugar from an airtight container into the bowl of her weighing scales, wishing she was somewhere other than the Marriotts' expensively appointed kitchen. More specifically, she wishes she was where she ought to have been tonight; in her boyfriend Mickey's dingy Whitechapel bedsit, sprawled out on his bed with his shaven head buried between her splayed thighs. Mickey's been on the road all week, taking a delivery of car parts over to a factory in Bremen, and when he's been cooped up in his truck, deprived of Lena's company for a few days, he's always extra pleased to see her. And that, more often than not, translates as a long slow session of oral gratification – the gratification being mostly Lena's, as she comes again and again on his twisting, probing, licking tongue.

But she's had to cancel her plans for tonight because Hillary Marriott needs some help in the kitchen. No, make that a lot of help. Hillary barely has the culinary knowhow to boil an egg, which is why she's asked Lena to stay beyond her agreed hours and produce some iced fancies for the coffee morning she's throwing tomorrow. It's to raise money for the local hospice, a particularly worthy cause in the eyes of Hillary's social set, and she wants everyone to think the selection of cakes on offer is all her own work.

It's not the first time Lena has been required to save her employer's blushes in this way, and she knows there'll be a little something extra in her pay packet come the end of the week, but she can't help feeling resentful at having to give up her longed-for night with Mickey. At least she can channel her feelings of disappointment into her baking, beating the icing sugar with cream cheese to make frosting for the buns that currently sit on the top shelf of the oven, filling the kitchen with a delicious vanilla aroma as they cook.

Grating lemon zest to add to the frosting, Lena lets her thoughts drift back to Mickey. Her friends have never understood what she sees in him; they think he's dull and uncouth, and they think she should look for a lover who'll improve her social standing. Hillary's husband, Paul, is something to do with mergers and acquisitions in the City; he must have plenty of suitable colleagues,

189

they say. Rich, single colleagues, some of them, who could treat Lena in the manner she deserves. She can't deny that would be nice, especially if they have the same cultured good looks and ingrained charm as Paul Marriott. But looks and charm – even money and all the trappings of a high-flying lifestyle – would, in the long term, be no compensation for what Mickey gives her. He knows what she really needs to keep her happy. Rough, uncompromising sex and a firm hand on her backside whenever she behaves like a brat.

Which reminds her, it's been far too long since Mickey gave her a damn good spanking. He's been working all the overtime he can get, trying to put some money aside so they can have a few days away together, somewhere in the sun. Maybe visit a resort with a naturist beach like they sometimes talk about, though in her fantasies she's always the only one who's naked, bared and displayed for a group of faceless men who all want to spank and fuck her.

The thought brings a smile to Lena's lips and a pleasing dampness to her pussy. Lost in an erotic daydream where too many cocks to count plough into her wet depths, fucking her fiercely from behind so that every thrust brings their groins hard into contact with her sore, freshly punished backside, Lena doesn't register at first that the kitchen no longer smells of vanilla and warm sugar. Instead, there's a distinct, unpleasant aroma of something burning.

With a despairing moan, Lena grabs oven gloves and dives for the oven. Pulling out the tray of buns, she sees that every last one is blackened on top. Maybe they're still salvageable, she tells herself; maybe she can slice off the tops and plaster them so thickly with frosting no one will ever know the difference. Yes, that might work. All she has to do is let them cool off a little, then get a sharp knife and …

That's the precise moment Hillary Marriott chooses to walk into the kitchen to find out how Lena's getting on.

Her retroussé nose – fashioned by one of the most exclusive surgeons on Harley Street, Hillary having very little of her original face left, as Lena knows from the wedding photos hidden away in the guest room – wrinkles at the smell of charred sponge cake. The smile fades from her perfectly made-up face.

'Goodness me, Lena. Those buns aren't burned, are they?'

There's no point lying. Hillary's clearly had so many kitchen disasters of her own, she can't fail to notice someone else's.

'Yes, Mrs Marriott. But only a little bit. I should be able to get rid of the worst parts –'

Her employer cuts her off sharply. 'And serve substandard cakes to my guests? What are you thinking, girl? I want you to start again and make a fresh batch of buns.'

Lena sneaks a glance at the clock on the wall, positioned just above the kitchen door. She'd been aiming to get away in the next ten minutes, once she'd iced the buns and done the last of the washing-up, but starting again from scratch means she'll be here for the best part of another hour. By the time she reaches Mickey's place, he'll be sound asleep, worn out by his long drive back from Germany. And, once Mickey's sleeping, he's almost impossible to rouse. She's tried it before, slipping down under the covers and taking his limp cock in her mouth, sucking hard in what proved to be a futile attempt to wake him. No, there'll be no fun for her tonight, and she can't prevent a frustrated whine escaping from her lips.

'Is there a problem, Lena?' Hillary's tone drips ice. She's a reasonable boss – God knows Lena's worked for far worse, and walked out on most of them within a fortnight – but she expects to have her instructions carried out with no complaints.

'No, Mrs Marriott,' Lena replies. 'It's just … I was hoping I could leave soon, that was all.'

'And leave me in the lurch, embarrass me in front of my guests, is that the case?'

'Not at all.' Lena can't understand why Hillary is being so awkward tonight. It's only a tray of buns, when all's said and done. There's any number of artisan bakeries in this part of West London who'd provide a dozen red velvet cupcakes or an iced Genoese sponge at a moment's notice. Though maybe their offerings wouldn't look homemade enough; wouldn't give the impression that Hillary's gone to any trouble for tomorrow's little *kaffee-klatsch*. And that would never do. 'I'll stay and make some more cakes, Mrs Marriott, honestly I will.'

'Yes, you will.' And now Lena hears something new in Hillary Marriott's voice; something her imagination, already overheated by the fantasies that caused her to let the buns burn in the first place, seizes on as a dominant overtone. 'You'll stay, and you'll learn what happens when you try to disobey my orders.'

How, Lena wonders, did this turn into a matter of 'disobedience' and 'orders'? And why is her pussy suddenly flooding with sticky juice at what Hillary's choice of words implies?

'Are you saying you're going to punish me?' Lena can't quite believe she's asking the question, almost provoking her employer into a response.

Hillary shakes her head, ash-blonde bob shining in the fluorescent light. 'No, I'm not saying that.'

For a moment, Lena feels hollow, unaccountably let down, even though she knows it was only her lust-driven imagination that placed her over Hillary's knee, bottom bared for a spanking she almost, but not quite, deserves.

There's a strange smile on Hillary's lips, hovering somewhere between cruelty and amusement. 'Because I'm going to let Paul do it.'

'Mr Marriott?' Lena looks round, thinking she should be making herself useful with eggs and butter, attempting to replace the buns she's just ruined, rather than staring foolishly at Hillary, not sure if she's heard the woman correctly. It's as though her world is a snowglobe and someone's just turned it upside down, setting everything it contains whirling madly around her.

'You see, Lena, Paul and I have been talking about this for quite some time.' Hillary steps closer. Lena can smell her perfume – something by Chanel that costs as much for the big bottle sitting on Hillary's dressing table as she herself earns in a week. Underneath its floral, feminine bouquet, Lena thinks she detects a whiff of something more earthy and ripe. If it wasn't all so unlikely, she'd swear her employer was turned on by what's happening here.

'Really?' Lena fiddles with an unused wooden spoon, just for something to do to break the growing tension.

'Oh, yes. On the whole, Lena, we're pleased with the job you do as our housekeeper, but we've both been feeling for some time that, if you're not subject to a certain amount of supervision, you have a tendency to ... slack off.'

A guilty flush rises to Lena's face. Most of the time she works hard, as is expected of her, but sometimes she can't resist taking ten minutes longer on her coffee break than she really ought, or leaving without sorting the rubbish into the various recycling bins provided by the local council. How does Hillary know this? Have she and Paul been spying on her? She's heard of households where they put a teddy bear with a built-in camera into the nursery, to make sure the nanny isn't mistreating the children. Maybe they've done the same to her, hiding the camera in the bedroom, so they can catch her dabbing herself with Hillary's expensive scent before she goes off to meet Mickey. God, what if they were recording footage of her the afternoon she tried on all the evening dresses in Hillary's wardrobe, parading in front of the mirror and admiring the way the velvet and lace confections clung to her curves? Her mind runs away with her, imagining all the reasons they could find to relieve her of her duties.

'I'm sorry, Mrs Marriott.' Lena tugs nervously at the end of the plait she's twisted her long black hair into, wondering if she'll find herself looking for a new job tomorrow. 'It won't happen again, I promise.'

'Of course,' Hillary continues, 'we did consider whether it was worth keeping you on ...' Her pause is long enough to make Lena dread what might be coming next. 'But you're courteous, you're not light-fingered – unlike that dreadful girl from Tallinn we had the misfortune to hire – and –' she glances briefly at the blackened buns in their non-stick tray '– the odd little mishap notwithstanding, you're the best cook we've ever employed. So we decided that we'd keep an eye on you, and, if you ever did anything that might, in other circumstances, lead to your dismissal, we'd find some other method of dealing with it.'

Is the woman spinning her a line? Lena can't believe that failing to keep an eye on the oven for five minutes is a sackable offence, no matter how strict an employer might be. Indeed, she's starting to think the Marriotts have cooked up this whole scheme to spank her on a whim, then simply looked for the first opportunity to put it into practice. She has to admire their deviousness, even as she tries to ignore the heat building between her legs and the nervous excitement swirling in her belly at the thought of receiving punishment for this minor misdeed.

Realising Hillary Marriott is waiting for her to respond, she murmurs, 'I understand, and I appreciate that you have the right to punish me in whichever way you see fit.'

'I knew you'd see it that way, Lena.' Hillary licks her small, coral-glossed lips. 'Paul!' she calls through the open doorway.

Within moments, her husband appears, casually dressed in a navy rollneck sweater and jeans and carrying a copy of the evening paper, as though he's been interrupted in the act of reading it. Lena suppresses a shiver of regret that he isn't in his work suit; there's something so deliciously humiliating about being over the knee of a formally dressed man, waiting for him to begin spanking you. And she has no doubt this is where he intends to place her within the next few moments.

'Ah, Lena, I understand my wife has reason to be displeased with your work.' Paul's smile is kinder than his wife's, deep wrinkles appearing at the corners of his brown eyes. Lena might like her men on the rough and ready side, with work-callused hands and brawny bodies like Mickey's, but she can't deny Paul Marriott has a certain appeal. Polite, handsome – and with a deviant streak to his personality, which seems, the more she stares at the two of them, ideally attuned to that of his wife. Oh, they make a perfect pair. Why has she never realised it till now?

'Yes, that's right, sir.' Usually, she calls him 'Mr Marriott', but tonight she can't help but refer to him by the honorific. It seems right, somehow; appropriate given the situation.

'Would you care to explain to me what caused all this?' He sets the paper down on the kitchen table, folded so she can see part of the front-page headline. The word 'CRACKDOWN' screams out at her; it makes her think of what his palm will soon be doing on her backside, and she feels the urge to giggle. The stern expression on Paul Marriott's face quickly stifles that urge.

'I burned the buns that were supposed to be for Mrs Marriott's coffee morning tomorrow, sir.'

'Really? An expert cook like you?' he comments. 'And just how did you let that happen?'

'I – I was daydreaming when I should have been watching the time, sir.'

'Oh, Lena, I really would have expected better of you.'

How does he know what to expect? she asks herself. He's never here during the day, never sees me hard at work vacuuming the floor or scrubbing the en suite toilet. This is all just a performance – and he's very good at it. Just the right tone of sorrow and regret, giving the impression he really doesn't want to treat her so severely but knows any chastisement will be for her own good. He must have done this before, but she doesn't want to speculate when, or to whom. All she knows with any certainty is that his wife has never been on the receiving end of one of his punishments. They're both tops, and that's why they need a willing bottom to be the third party in their scene. Someone just like Lena.

With an effort, trying not to think just how willing and eager she is to give herself up to Marriott's punishing palm, she responds to his words of reproach. 'I know, and I'm sorry, sir.'

'So, tell me, Lena, what kind of daydream would cause you to forget you had a tray of cakes in the oven?'

She could lie, but there's something cathartic about admitting she's been having horny fantasies on her employers' time. 'I was thinking about all the things I'm going to let my boyfriend do to me the next time I see him.' When his eyebrows quirk upwards, she realises he wants her to elaborate. 'He's very good with his tongue,' she admits, 'and he licks me till I've had so many orgasms I just can't take it any more.'

'Does he ever spank you?' Marriott asks.

'Only when I deserve it, sir.'

'Just like you do now ...' As he speaks, Marriott reaches for one of the stripped-pine kitchen chairs, and pulls it away from the table and into the centre of the granite-tiled floor.

His wife says nothing, clearly letting him run this scene for the time being. Lena senses she'll step in when the moment is right.

Sitting, spreading his legs apart wide enough for her to see the distinct bulge that's formed at his crotch, he pats his left thigh, silently demanding she drape herself over it. Without hesitation, she does as he asks, even though she knows just how humiliating it is to place herself in this position.

Marriott runs his hand over her bottom, covered by the short blue uniform dress she's required to wear while performing her duties in this house. With its neat white collar and cuffs, it usually makes her feel confident and professional. Now, she's achingly aware that all she wears under it is a pair of plain white nylon panties.

'Are you ready for this?' Marriott asks, the flat of his hand in the small of Lena's back, holding her steady.

'Yes, sir.' Lena's voice is small, tight. Fear makes a knot in her throat, but lower down her body is alive to the prospect of the pain – and, she is sure, pleasure – to come.

'Just a minute,' Hillary pipes up. 'Rather than use your hand, Paul, wouldn't it be more appropriate to punish Lena with this?'

Lena raises her head to see Hillary brandishing a wooden spoon, and a sick thrill runs through her. Though she's often fantasised about being paddled, or striped with Mickey's belt, he's never used anything other than his hand on her. However hard he hits her with that, she knows she can take it. She could take Marriott's palm with similar ease. The spoon, however, is another matter.

'What an outstanding idea.' Marriott's tone is full of admiration for his wife's ingenuity.

Hillary hands over the spoon, and a moment later Lena feels Marriott tapping it gently against her bum cheek. 'So,' he says. 'You ruined a dozen buns, so a dozen strokes would be fair punishment, don't you think?'

'Whatever you decide, sir.' All Lena wants now is for him to get this over with, but he seems in no hurry to land the first blow. Instead, he inches up the hem of her dress, until she can feel the cool air of the kitchen on her panty-clad backside.

'Very nice,' he mutters, and she swears she feels his cock swelling beneath her, pushing at the fly of his jeans.

Without warning, the spoon whistles through the air, slamming down against the fleshiest part of Lena's arse. It takes a moment for the actual pain to register, and, when it does, she utters a shocked yelp. Marriott ignores her, concentrating on dishing out another equally stinging blow. And another, and another.

He hasn't asked her to count, but, even as she writhes on his lap, begging for mercy, she's doing her best to keep track of the strokes. Somewhere to the left of her, Hillary is crooning, 'Oh, yes, that's it. Give her what she deserves, Paul.'

Head down, Lena can't see what the woman is doing, but the rustling noises and the occasional sigh she hears suggests Hillary may have her fingers buried in her panties and is bringing herself off.

She can't be certain, but she thinks she's taken six swats of the spoon. Her counting seems to tally with Marriott's because he pauses and says, 'Halfway there, Lena. You're taking these very well. But let's see what happens when those panties of yours come down ...'

'Please, sir. Please don't pull them down,' Lena begs, but he hooks his fingers into the waistband, ruthlessly pulling her underwear down past the crease where her buttocks meet her thighs. The wetness in the gusset must be apparent to him, and he chuckles at her neediness.

She knows she must look foolish, bottom bared in this way, and she can't begin to imagine what shade of red her skin has gone. The pain is worse than she expected, but, beneath it, pleasure is beginning to make its sweet presence felt. *I can take this*, she assures herself.

And, somehow, she does, even though her yelps have turned to full-throated cries and tears are filling her eyes and threatening to spill down on to her cheeks. Paul is ruthless in her punishment, but, as he nears the end of the dozen strokes, he pauses to run a hand into Lena's soaking cleft. When he brushes his finger over the point of her clit, she grinds herself against his thighs, unable to hold back. Just a little more of that teasing friction would be enough to have her coming, but he denies her that fulfilment. Still two strokes to go, and now he really lays them on, spanking her so hard he threatens to snap the spoon in half. Even as she jerks on his lap like a puppet whose strings have been severed, driven to distraction by the pain in her arse, Lena feels a quiet triumph at having taken everything Marriott had to give.

'Oh, God, that's it!' Lena hears Hillary groan as the last of the punishment is delivered, and knows the woman has reached her own orgasm. Glancing up, vision blurred by tears, she sees her normally prim and proper employer lost in erotic abandon, churning her fingers furiously in her panties as she comes. It's an image that will stay with her long after she leaves the house tonight.

Though she has the feeling that won't be for quite a while yet.

Marriott lets the spoon drop to the floor with a sharp clattering sound, then eases Lena off his lap. Roughly, he yanks open the poppers running down the front of her dress and pushes it off her shoulders, stripping her naked. Urging her to take a kneeling position between his spread thighs, he unzips his fly and reaches in to free his cock.

It's mouth-wateringly big, with a blunt, circumcised head, and Lena needs no persuasion to wrap her fingers round it.

'Ooh, you're going to make her suck your cock, aren't you?' Hillary moans, and Lena glances over long enough to assure herself that the woman's fingers are buried deep in her pussy once more, their rapid movement obvious through the lace front of Hillary's panties. 'Make her get it nice and wet, so it'll slide into her arse easily ...'

Lena's only just beginning to realise quite how perverse the Marriotts' desires are, and how much fun she's going to have fulfilling all of them. She wouldn't be surprised if she has to use her lips and tongue on Hillary, too, before the night is over, a prospect that doesn't faze her in the slightest, particularly if she gets to smear the woman's pussy beforehand with some of that lemon frosting still sitting neglected on the kitchen table.

Kneeling on the floor, relishing the dull ache in her

freshly punished arse, Lena's last thought before she plunges her mouth down on Marriott's straining shaft is that she was supposed to be whipping up a fresh batch of buns before she leaves. Oh, well, she thinks, it looks like Hillary's going to be taking a delivery from the local baker in advance of her coffee morning, after all ...

THE SILVER CHAIN – PRIMULA BOND

Good things come to those who wait…

After a chance meeting one evening, mysterious entrepreneur Gustav Levi and photographer Serena Folkes agree to a very special contract.

Gustav will launch Serena's photographic career at his gallery, but only if Serena agrees to become his companion.

To mark their agreement, Gustav gives Serena a bracelet and silver chain which binds them physically and symbolically. A sign that Serena is under Gustav's power.

As their passionate relationship intensifies, the silver chain pulls them closer together. But will Gustav's past tear them apart?

A passionate, unforgettable erotic romance for fans of *50 Shades of Grey* and Sylvia Day's *Crossfire Trilogy*.

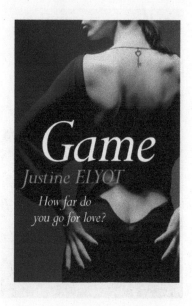

GAME – JUSTINE ELYOT

The stakes are high, the game is on.

In this sequel to Justine Elyot's bestselling *On Demand*, Sophie discovers a whole new world of daring sexual exploits.

Sophie's sexual tastes have always been a bit on the wild side – something her boyfriend Lloyd has always loved about her.

But Sophie gives Lloyd every part of her body except her heart. To win all of her, Lloyd challenges Sophie to live out her secret fantasies.

As the game intensifies, she experiments with all kinds of kinks and fetishes in a bid t understand what she really wants. But Lloyd feature in her final decision? Or will the ultimate risk he takes drive her away from him?

Find out more at www.mischiefbooks.com

POWER PLAY – CHARLOTTE STEIN

Now she's the boss, everything that once seemed forbidden is possible…

Meet Eleanor Harding, a woman who loves to be in control and who puts Anastasia Steele in the shade.

When Eleanor is promoted, she loses two very important things: the heated relationship she had with her boss, and control over her own desires.

She finds herself suddenly craving something very different – and office junior, Ben, seems like just the sort of man to fulfil her needs. He's willing to show her all of the things she's been missing – namely, what it's like to be the one in charge.

Now all Eleanor has to do is decide…is Ben calling the kinky shots, or is she?

Find out more at www.mischiefbooks.com

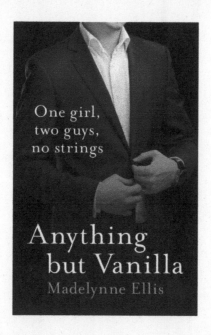

ANYTHING BUT VANILLA
MADELYNNE ELLIS

One girl, two guys, no strings.

Kara North is on the run. Fleeing from her controlling fiancé and a wedding she never wanted, she accepts the chance offer of refuge on Liddell Island, where she soon catches the eye of the island's owner, erotic photographer Ric Liddell.

But pleasure comes in more than one flavour when Zachary Blackwater, the charming ice-cream vendor also takes an interest, and wants more than just a tumble in the surf.

When Kara learns that the two men have been unlikely lovers for years, she becomes obsessed with the idea of a threesome.

Soon Kara is wondering how she ever considered committing herself to just one man.

Find out more at www.mischiefbooks.com